CASINO DE FRANCE

GRAHAM TEMPEST

BRIGHTWAY PRESS

Oliver Steele & Kon Feaver thrillers:

CASINO CARIBBEAN

CASINO DE FRANCE

CASINO HAVANA

FEAVER PITCH

JOBURG STEELE

CASINO QADDAFI

Brightway Press, 522 Hunt Club Blvd., Apopka, Florida 32703
bp#260614b

1

———

Paris, October 1st 2015

Fredy stepped out of the shower and twirled before a mirror in the sixth floor penthouse on Île Saint-Louis.

Katerina walked by. Taking a towel, she flicked it at his behind. It snicked the flesh and he winced.

His ebony body was in good shape for thirty, he thought, just a slight rounding of the stomach. There were so many good restaurants in Paris. But he wasn't going to let the odd extra pound bother him; his appeal to women owed more to a generous budget than to his physique.

Katrina was dressed to go out. Her skinny jeans, baggy sweater and huge dark glasses said famous fashion model trying to be anonymous but not trying too hard.

"Where are you going?" he asked.

"Out."

"Will you be long?"

"A couple of hours. I'm meeting Rudi at Le Printemps. We'll probably grab a sandwich." Rudi was her agent.

He grunted, expressionless. "Be careful."

"I'm always careful."

The year 2015 had been a year of terrorism in France.

There was the killing in January of twelve people in the office of the satirical magazine Charlie Hebdo. Four customers of a kosher market were shot a few days later. Then in August there was the attempted terrorist attack on a Paris-bound train. It had made people nervous.

But it was fair to say that Katerina and the people in her world had not been much affected, such was the blinkered community of high fashion. Their self-centred lives rolled on as if nothing had happened.

Katerina was not sure what to make of Fredy. They had hit it off when they met three months ago and had been together constantly since, but she still felt she barely knew him.

She knew what everyone knew: he was the son of the president of the oil-rich Kongolo Republic in Central Africa. The newspapers portrayed him as a playboy, a fast car lover and a spendthrift. He was educated at Oxford –

briefly – and Los Angeles, where he was currently enrolled at Pepperdine University, although some sniped that he lacked the desire to read a book unless it was pornography, or about cars.

There were other stories. His father's rise to power in Kongolo had reportedly involved murder, torture and even cannibalism. There were rumours that the son was just as ruthless as his father, and possibly with a crazier streak.

She hadn't seen anything like that. There would always be stuff in the tabloids, mostly made up. Besides, she liked him. He might not be the world's most articulate person but he had a dry sense of humour. And he was free with money, showering her with gifts.

So when the French government confiscated his family's huge mansion on Avenue Victor Hugo – something about a money-laundering probe – she had let him move in. She found him physically attractive. He was her type she thought, amused at her own vulgarity.

She picked up her purse and made for the door but he grabbed her from behind. She could feel his arousal.

She giggled and pulled away. "I'm late."

The door slammed and she was gone.

Well if that was how she was going to treat him. He found his mobile phone and chose a number on speed-dial.

"Come round in ten minutes," he said. "Both of you."

The he made a call to an Algerian called Zidane in a flat in a drab part of the 14th Arrondissement. He had not added the number to his phone directory, preferring to memorise it.

"I've thought about your request. I will do it. Do you want euros or dollars?"

The reply seemed to satisfy him.

He listened for several minutes, then said, "Given the size of the blast I'll need to be far away when it happens – just like you, my friend!"

Finally, "Text me an account and a routing number. The funds will be wired by the weekend."

Zidane texted the information to him a few minutes later.

Fredy was used to moving money around the world. He telephoned the Consolidated Bank of Africa where he kept a major balance on current account and identified himself, using a password. He gave the necessary instructions. Then, confident that the money would be in Zidane's account by the next day, he poured himself a large scotch, walked to the window overlooking Paris and sat down to think.

He was indifferent to the fate of Jews or Muslims. He was Roman Catholic himself and nominal at that. But he did have a burning resentment of the French government. It was branded deep in his soul. Now events were making it possible for him to do something about it.

The buzzer sounded downstairs and he admitted the

caller to the building. Moments later the flat's bell chimed. Winding a towel around his waist, he went to the door.

Two women entered, smiling. One was oriental, the other blonde with high cheekbones and flat features from east of the Urals. Both wore tight dresses with short skirts. In heavy makeup and shiny jewellery, they were dressed more for evening than for the middle of the day.

The blonde looked him up and down, and laughed. "What a man you are, to be sure."

"What's your name?" he asked, his voice rough with excitement.

She smiled. "Tania."

Taking her hand, he led her to a sofa facing the big full-length window that overlooked the Seine.

She shot a sideways glance at her friend, giving her a wink. Then, because she was a good natured girl who liked to please, she commenced to moan and writhe convincingly as Fredy set to work.

2

OCTOBER 8TH

Following orders, I walked into the Hôtel Meurice at cocktail time on a rainy Paris evening.

Kathy came out to the lobby and beckoned. "We're in the bar."

Kathy is blonde, five seven and cute. Not skinny but not fat either. She is twenty-seven or twenty-eight – she did tell me but I always forget – with blonde hair down to her shoulders, jeans and a crisp Miami Heat T-shirt. She was wearing bright pink sneakers which you might think wouldn't cut it in Paris but somehow they seemed to work. Must be the smile.

My client Carlton Tisch is a connoisseur of expensive hotels, so when he summoned me to the French capital I was not surprised to find the little financier well ensconced at the Hôtel Meurice with Mimi, his child bride.

Mimi is not really a child, she's twenty-five but alongside grey-haired Tisch, who is sixty, she sometimes looks that way. She and Kathy are friends.

Tisch nodded, unsmiling. "What's your poison, young man?"

The girls were sipping martinis and Tisch was nursing a tall glass of beer. At home on Tortola, he swigs Red Stripe beer from the can but I suppose even he didn't have the nerve to do that in the baroque luxury of the Meurice. I ordered a Mojito.

The waiter brought my drink, his look taking in Tisch and the young women with approval. Tisch noticed and was visibly pleased.

There was something going on but I had no idea what. Before I could ask, in strolled Kon Feaver, grinning. Kon, who is Israeli, always looks as if he has just walked off a kibbutz although he's never worked a day down on the farm. He's solidly built, muscular and leathery with a lived-in forty year old face. He lives in a cabin in the Florida Keys and we sometimes fish together. His past includes playing soccer for Tel Aviv and spending time as a pilot in the Israeli air force, cut short by heavy drinking. That's behind him now, he says, but he still casts a wistful glance at a well-stocked bar.

"I see everyone's here," he said cheerfully.

Tisch shook his head. "One more to come."

"Who?"

"Someone called Saadi."

"Egyptian?"

"Moroccan."

Tisch sipped his beer. He is taciturn to a fault. Finally my impatience got the better of me.

"Spit it out. Why are we here?"

Shaven headed Saadi trotted along the rain-slicked Rue de Rivoli like the White Rabbit, checking his watch. It was cool and just getting dark. The expensive little shops were set back under a protective arcade but he had to cross the road from the Metro, getting wet as he did so. As he entered the Meurice, he wiped the moisture from his head with a tissue.

The terrorist Zidane followed him in the street. When Saadi turned into the hotel, Zidane walked straight by so as not to be noticed. He stopped twenty yards later opposite the window of an expensive boutique, and showed sudden interest in some diamond-studded pumps on a stand.

A man, presumably Saadi entered the bar.

"Here he is." Tisch stood and waved him to the sofa. He perched nervously between Kathy and Mimi.

Nobody thought to offer him a drink. A cloud of separateness hovered over his damp head.

"You look like a terrorist, you should let your hair grow," barked Tisch.

Saadi just smiled. "I couldn't be a terrorist, I lack the passion."

"What do you do?" I asked.

"I write computer programs."

"Among other things," said Kathy.

"You can talk in front of Oliver," said Tisch. "He works for me."

I resented that. I actually work for myself, but I let it pass.

"Saadi doesn't just write code," said Tisch. "He works for Solly Goldhawk, looking for investment opportunities."

I had heard of Goldhawk, an Anglo-French entrepreneur. Years ago he made a fortune on the London Stock Exchange and eloped with an Italian heiress, causing a huge scandal. He was known for spotting business trends well ahead of the general public. Was Saadi one of his research tools?

"Are you an industrial spy?" I asked.

Saadi laughed. "Not a terrorist, but *un espion*? Yes, guilty."

Tisch said, "Through his work, Saadi has just come across some peculiar transactions, suggesting radical Islam. He told Goldhawk and Goldhawk told me."

"Why you?" I asked.

"Goldhawk and I are friends, and we both deplore religious extremism."

"Amen to that, but why didn't Solly go to the authorities?"

No reply. I guessed the real reason was that anything told to a government agency, particularly in the wake of Charlie Hebdo, would probably leak to the press. Tisch and Goldhawk were both controlling individuals who liked to work quietly, out of the public eye. The media's heavy-footedness would be unwelcome.

"How did you come upon this information?" I asked Saadi.

"I monitor bank metadata. It's part of my job."

"Isn't metadata non-specific?" I said. "It doesn't tell you what messages say, only that they took place. That's what Homeland Security says, so I guess it's true."

"I drill down into the data."

"Really?" I was starting to suspect that 'bank security' was something of an oxymoron.

He hesitated. "If you run that information against other databases you sometimes see relationships."

"Relationships?"

"One of them is Zidane," said Tisch.

There was silence.

Terrorism has generated its own folk heroes and Zidane is one of them.

In the seventies, a rabid Marxist-Leninist known as Carlos the Jackal committed a series of daring raids. He was eventually caught and imprisoned for life but a certain romantic image persists. Zidane is Carlos' successor in terms of notoriety. He's still at large.

He is French Algerian and also speaks English, German, Italian and Arabic. He studied engineering at London University but was expelled for his racist views. He's also a bomb-maker; his signature has been detected in numerous suicide bombings.

"Zidane is receiving money?" I asked.

"Correct."

"How much?"

"Two million dollars."

"Who from?"

"I'm working on that," said Saadi. "I should know soon."

"It's important," I said.

"Why wait?" groused Tisch. "Obviously there's something heavy going down." He watches a lot of television.

"Where do I fit in?" I asked. "If neither the CIA nor the *Sûreté* can find Zidane, I doubt if I can."

Tisch nodded. "But you might be able to trace whoever is paying him."

"Let's talk when you know where the money is coming from," I said to Saadi.

"Got it," said Saadi. He stood up. He looked uneasy in the Meurice's stifling luxury.

I knew how he felt. I myself had booked a room at the Hôtel des Saints-Pères on the Left Bank. It was a traditional hotel with a charming courtyard at a fraction of the cost of the Meurice. Carlton wouldn't have been seen dead there.

After Saadi left, we sipped our drinks.

"Nice guy," I said.

"Your crack about terrorism was tactless," Mimi said to her husband. "Him being an Arab."

Tisch shrugged.

"Why do the terrorists target Paris rather than other places?" asked Kathy.

Some women look great in a T-shirt and Kathy is one. It seems to go with the wholesome American girl thing. She must have just showered because her hair was damp, making it look darker, but her arms were golden brown. She was a real beach blonde.

"France has the largest Muslim population in Europe," I said.

"Does that answer the question?"

"Many of them live in concrete slums on the outskirts of the city – depressing places."

"But they have the same rights as other French people, don't they?"

"With exceptions."

"Such as?"

"It's illegal in France to wear any "ostentatious" sign of religion in a public space – at a school, a post office or any federal building. That includes Christian crucifixes, Jewish yarmulkes – skullcaps – and Muslim hijabs."

Mimi wagged a finger at her husband. "Remember not to wear a yarmulke in a French Post Office, Carlton."

"Wouldn't want to."

I changed the subject. "Why does Carlton piss away a fortune staying in these posh places?" I asked Mimi. I didn't bother to keep my voice down.

She smiled. "Do you know the history of this hotel?"

"No."

"This is where General von Choltitz, the military governor of Paris, stayed during the Second World War."

"It was the German headquarters?"

She nodded. "Choltitz was an unusual character. He's credited with disobeying a direct order from Hitler to destroy Paris in 1944. Instead, he surrendered it to the Free French."

"So he's a hero to the French?"

"To some extent. But he was also responsible for the deaths of several thousand Jews at the siege of Sebastopal, so he was a bit of a mixed bag."

"What happened to Carlton's family during the war?" I asked. "I thought they moved to America long before that."

"His grandparents immigrated, but various uncles and aunts stayed in Germany."

"So he has cousins there?"

"All dead."

I looked over at Carlton. "Sorry."

"He stays here whenever he's in town," said Mimi. "Sometimes I think he invents reasons to visit Paris just because of that. It's about living well being the best revenge."

Carlton was busy with his beer.

When Saadi left the hotel, he turned left and walked towards Tuileries metro station. He was in a better mood after sharing his story. He was already thinking about algorithms that he could use to yield the information he had promised Oliver. Zidane, un-noticed, fell in behind him.

Saadi arrived at the art deco subway station entrance and inserted his magnetic pass. In the warm, disinfected air, he descended a dozen steps to the platform, shoulder to shoulder with jostling Parisians intent on getting home after work.

As he waited for the train that would take him to his small flat south of Montparnasse, he moved towards the edge of the platform, hoping to get a seat when the train arrived.

In the press of people, he barely felt the pinprick but it caused an instant attack of dizziness and he sagged back against the person behind him, who put out an arm in support.

A rushing wind swelled from the black mouth of the tunnel, preceding the train. The crowd instinctively moved a step or two back from the edge but the person supporting Saadi pushed him forwards. As if swooning, he toppled onto the rail in front of the train.

Amid the shocked cries of the crowd, Zidane slipped quietly away.

Kongolo, Central Africa, August 13th

François Mifuba, President of the Republic of Kongolo, cut off a bloody piece of steak and chewed it. It was the best filet, imported from Zimbabwe.

He bared his teeth and smiled at his Vice President who stood in front of him.

"Delicious."

"Yes, excellency."

"Reminds me of that opposition leader I deposed in 1998. I don't recall his name, but I never forget a taste."

"Yes, excellency."

It was the only safe reply. The President's sense of humour was often macabre but one never quite knew if he was joking.

The small African in a dark suit was well aware of the

rumour that he was a cannibal; that he ate the flesh of his enemies as a way of imbibing their strength. It wasn't true, but he never denied it; it didn't hurt to have a few grisly tales circulating.

He frowned and looked at his watch.

"Josephson is late!"

"Yes, excellency."

Josephson was one of the few people in his country that Mifuba could not control. He was the general manager of Lorraine Petroleum, the French oil giant that managed the Kongolo oil reserves. He was probably coming to complain about the money the President had been siphoning away from the refinery and into his own pocket.

Well, they would see about that.

Mifuba had assumed power twenty years ago after having his uncle shot. He ran the country as a kleptocracy with himself as chief kleptocrat, diverting much of the country's oil revenue into his own coffers.

A servant appeared.

"Monsieur Josephson is here."

The tall Frenchman in pressed grey slacks and open-necked shirt was formally dressed by jungle standards, but he looked casual beside Mifuba who was always immaculate, changing his white shirt several times a day.

"Good morning, Monsieur President."

He towered over the small man until Mifuba motioned him to sit down.

"You asked to see me," growled the president. "What's the problem?"

Josephson cleared his throat. He had prepared for this meeting, but the little dictator always made him nervous. There were those rumours.

"Sir, the refinery badly needs repairs. Your cash demands have left it in constant deficit."

"So you have said many times. Do you take me for a savage, with your artful figures?"

Josephson flushed. That was pretty much how Lorraine Petroleum's directors did view Mifuba, although they would never admit it.

"Machinery wears out fast in the humidity here."

Mifuba scowled. That at least was true. Kongolo enjoyed a combination of extreme weather and absence of a trained workforce, the worst possible environment for machinery.

Josephson went on. "And with the decline in oil prices, it's difficult to compete in world markets."

Mifuba stood up. He had expected to be lied to, and Josephson was not disappointing him.

"Your prices are hedged for years ahead, so that argument is false," said Mifuba.

Josephson felt his cheeks burn. In his haste to make a point he had been caught in a lie. But he was only doing the bidding of his employers – the oil company and the French government that controlled it.

"I understand, Sir. I didn't mean . . ."

Mifuba turned and marched away. Josephson spoke to his retreating back.

"I will report to my superiors."

"Do that," Mifuba growled.

Left alone, Josephson made his way out of the palace, watched by retainers. He felt relief as he emerged into the sunlight and climbed into his Citroen.

"Back to the refinery?" asked the driver, who was French.

"No," said Josephson. He gave another address. "That man gives me the creeps," he said .

Several times over the years, company employees had disappeared without explanation, their bodies never found. Responsibility was never traced to Mifuba but in each case the person in question had clashed with government officials.

Meanwhile, the refinery was being slowly but surely run into the ground.

Indoors, Mifuba bumped into his son.

Fredy nodded coolly at his father. "I won't see you for a while. I'm going to Paris."

Fredy was being educated in California – that is, he was partying, drinking and drugging his way through university, acquiring a knowledge of fast cars, opportunities for spending money and not much else. Regularly, as soon as school was out, he would head for Paris.

Mifuba grunted. "What will you be doing there?"

"The usual."

That meant womanising and spending money. The father owned a six floor mansion on Avenue Victor Hugo. He seldom used it but his son more or less lived there. He made no secret of the fact that Kongolo bored him. It had no social life and the primitive roads provided no scope for the expensive cars he kept in Paris.

Fredy left his father shaking his head and was driven to the private airstrip that had been carved out of the jungle a couple of miles from the presidential palace.

There he boarded a small jet, a Bombardier BD700 with a range of 6,000 miles. Piloted by two former Australian air force pilots, it would carry him nonstop to Paris without the inconvenience of rubbing shoulders with the common people.

The Citroen took Josephson to a smart residential area of the capital.

The two story houses were modern and many had air conditioning, in contrast to the rest of the city which consisted mostly of single story homes — large huts with jalousie windows and, if the owner was prosperous, a fan to circulate the air.

The Citroen stopped on an attractive street with a centre divider planted with shrubs and succulents.

Josephson marched up to the front door of a well-tended house and flung it open.

The young Kongolan woman inside smiled in welcome.

This was what had kept Josephson in Africa for five years – the ability to satisfy his appetites cheaply and often without needing to justify himself to anyone, least of all his wife who commanded their spacious home in the oil company camp and put on a good show as First Lady of the expatriate community.

The young woman came and put her arms around Josephson. She kissed him and started to lead him towards the bedroom but he tore off her outer clothing and threw her on the floor. She uttered a small cry and cringed in front of him – there was an element of role playing on her part but he was too excited to care.

Mifuba had listened to Josephson arguing about the need for repairs. The president was no fool but his mind was not attuned to that kind of logic. He had risen through political skill and ruthlessness, not attention to detail. He despised Josephson. The man was a glorified clerk.

But he saw that the Frenchman was spoiling for a fight. He could feel the resentment. There would be trouble there. The story about needing money for the refinery, well, of course he would say that and his fellow clerks at the top of the company would support him. Mifuba must pre-empt the situation.

He beckoned to the servant waiting on the far side of the room.

"Yes, Master?"

"Send Jules to me."

"Yes, Master."

Jules was Mifuba's bodyguard; from his appearance he could not be anything else. Aged forty, he was of medium height but broad. His short sleeved white shirt was stretched tight over muscular shoulders. There was a half-smile on his thick lipped face while a squashed nose suggested, correctly, that he had been a professional boxer.

He nodded easily at Mifuba. That in itself was unusual. Most people were afraid of the president, but in Jules's case, his skills were complementary to those of his country's leader and he could relax around him, knowing that he was perfectly qualified to carry out the kind of instructions he was used to receiving.

"Yes, Mr President?"

Mifuba beckoned him towards the window overlooking the palace forecourt.

"Do you see that man walking towards his car?"

"I do."

"Follow him."

"Sure. Anything else?"

Mifuba beckoned Jules closer to him and whispered in his ear.

Jules's smile grew broader. "Got it!"

. . .

Josephson was zipping up his trousers when the door opened. Jules stood in the doorway, watching him.

"Seen enough?" Josephson barked. "What the hell do you want?"

Jules smiled and produced a shiny automatic pistol, a Ruger. From his pocket he produced a silencer and deliberately screwed it onto the barrel. Josephson watched in disbelief.

"Look, this is a misunderstanding," he said. "If this lady is with you, I'm sorry."

"Misunderstanding? I suppose you could call it that." Jules' voice was as soft as velvet.

Josephson relaxed, gaining confidence. "Let's see if we can make this right." He reached for his wallet.

Jules held out his hand. "I'll take that."

Josephson gave him the wallet, reluctantly. Jules opened it with one hand, keeping his gun trained steadily on Josephson. There was a sheaf of banknotes inside. Jules teased them out with his teeth and tossed the wallet on the floor at Josephson's feet.

"See? No problem," said Josephson. He bent to pick up the wallet. As he leaned forward, Jules shot him in the forehead.

One shot was enough. The body fell to the floor.

The woman had watched in silence.

"He was a pig," she said. "You have done me a service. Can I repay the favour?"

She smiled.

"Not right now," said Jules. "But thanks for the offer." He aimed the gun at her and again a single shot was enough.

"No witnesses," he said under his breath. "If that's what the boss wants, that's what he gets."

Later that night there was a huge explosion in the refinery when an electrical fire broke out and spread to a tank of refined petroleum awaiting shipment to the port. Fourteen people were killed, ten Kongolans and four expatriate French. The fire burned for two days. By the time it was brought under control the damage was so great that the refinery was out of commission for a year.

Josephson's body was never found. He was blamed posthumously for the disaster, receiving no credit for his many warnings about the condition of the refinery. His widow, although she was ultimately successful, had to sue the company for his pension and death benefits.

4

Paris, October 8th

Kon waved to me after the meeting in the bar.

"Where are you staying?" I asked.

He grinned. "I have no idea. I don't fancy this place. Too grand for me."

"My thoughts too," I said. Why don't you stay at my hotel if they have room?"

"Which is?"

"The Hotel des Saints-Pères."

"Where is it?"

"On the left bank. The rooms are comfortable and there's a decent bar." I bit my lip but he grinned. "Deal. I'll see you there later."

· · ·

Kathy strolled over. I have to say her walk is a thing of beauty. Something about the motion of the hips, fluid and athletic in a healthy way rather than overtly sexy. But if you happen to find female athleticism sensuous, as I do, it ends up being erotic. She is also the right shape and size. Combine that with a restless intelligence and a mind that seems to move at the same speed as my own and you have a winning formula.

"Let's talk," she said. "Did you eat yet?"

We went to Brasserie Bofinger just off the Rue de la Bastille and I ordered onion soup.

I stirred the thin layer of grated Gruyere into the caramelised onions just beneath the surface of the hot broth. They merged into a white goop and I slurped a large spoonful. Delicious!

She said, "How are we going to play this?"

"We wait until we have some data to work with. Saadi seems smart, he should get us some useful stuff."

She shook her head. "Data, data! You are so data-oriented it makes me want to spit."

"How do you really feel?"

Kathy and I have an odd relationship. We have been teetering on the edge physically for some time now. If it were up to me, we would have gone over the edge long ago, but it isn't up to me. She sees to that.

"Let's consider this from the emotional angle," she said.

"What emotional angle? We don't have a starting point."

She talks a lot about emotion but she hasn't wasted much of it on me, unless her feelings are really well concealed.

"Even Zidane has emotions; they may be good or bad. Either way, they motivate him."

"I'm sure they do, but how? We have nothing to go on."

Kathy had ordered lobster salad and set about it with gusto. She tossed her blonde hair over her shoulders and ate, her face showing a range of expressions from thoughtful to amused – was that at me? – as I worked on my steak frites.

She changed direction suddenly. "What motivates you, Steele?"

"Whoa, what's up?"

"I mean here you are, six feet tall, not bad looking, you even show glimpses of a sense of humour occasionally."

"Thanks."

"You've had an expensive education, Oxford and that boarding school, what's it called, Pinnington?"

"Bunnington," I said. I enjoyed my days at Bunnington. They were part of a carefree time before life became complicated, before the troubles that led to my unwilling departure from the respectable areas of the accounting profession.

"Yeah. But with all those advantages you still have an emotional IQ of about sixty."

"And you base that observation on what?"

"Well, you haven't made a move on me, although you've had plenty of chances."

That came as a bit of a shock. Unless I missed all the signals, she has never shown me much encouragement.

"There was that time in California," I said.

"What time?"

"We spent the night together."

She gave me an old fashioned look. "You mean when your gay friend Magda looked in on us, so to speak?"

"Bi," I said automatically. My lodger Magda was unapologetically bisexual. I had a clear memory of the evening and I'm damn sure Kathy did too.

It happened when I was living in Santa Monica as caretaker of a house owned by Tisch. Kathy arrived from out of town and I finally managed to coax her into bed after a party, only to have the voluptuous Magda invite herself to join the fun. The result was an energetic night involving every permutation of three thoroughly tipsy people. A good time was had by all but it was a once-off and somehow none of us really felt like repeating the event.

"It doesn't count as a relationship if it's a threesome, is that what you're saying?" I asked.

"I guess I am, yeah." She looked at her watch. "Anyway, getting back to the business at hand, I intend to focus on the man's motivation. I think that should give us some insight into what he's planning to do."

"Focus away," I said. "I shall base my own efforts on the

computer information we get from Saadi about the money and its source. It's more efficient to work that way."

"For you," she said tartly.

"For me."

She didn't look as if she was going to pay the bill, so I settled it and we went back to the Meurice.

5

August 19th

Madame Marianne Caron, the French Minister of Energy, was puzzled.

She was reading a memo from an under-secretary about the fire that had devastated the Kongolo refinery a few days earlier.

At the bottom of the page, the under-secretary had written in blue ink: 'Time to nail this bastard.'

She wasn't offended by the salty language but she didn't understand the comment, so she picked up the phone. "*C'est Caron a l'appareil.* Please explain your rather emotional note."

He sounded apologetic. "I think we have a window of opportunity. The refinery will be closed for at least a year.

So, no matter how angry Mifuba gets at us, he can't cut off our oil supply because there *is* no oil supply. He has no leverage."

Caron was still not convinced. She had only been in office for a month. "Remind me why we don't like this guy?"

"He's a tyrant, as crooked as they come. He spends lavishly, launders money, treats his people like dirt."

"Forgive me, but is that unusual?"

The under-secretary laughed. "I suppose not. But he also kind of spits in our face."

"How so?"

"He has a big mansion on Avenue Victor Hugo and a bunch of cars that attract parking tickets by the hundred, never paid. His son is a flamboyant playboy who spends money like water here in Paris. It's not exactly good for our human rights image."

"So how should we proceed?"

"We should start a money-laundering investigation."

"Would that be successful?"

"Oh I think so. The Americans are already doing something similar. There were some suspicious transfers last year from Kongolo's oil accounts to a shell company in the Canary Islands, followed by purchases of beachfront property by the Mifubas. Some of the payments went through a Washington bank, and the Americans are using that as the hook for a money-laundering charge."

"In the United States."

"Yes. But I'm sure we could find similar transactions

here. We should start by investigating how they paid for the house on Victor Hugo. A French bank transfer was probably involved."

"Yes, for the house and the cars."

"Cars?" The under-secretary was dismissive. "Maybe, but it would be better to look for high value items."

Caron, who was a car enthusiast, said, "Do you know what a Bugatti Veyron costs?"

"I do not."

"Take a guess."

"I suppose they are expensive. Two hundred thousand euros?"

"Try two million. That's the base price. Custom paint is extra."

There was silence on the line.

In the weeks that followed, wheels were set in motion.

One day just before dawn a contingent of CRS, the Compagnies Républicaines de Sécurité, descended without warning on Avenue Victor Hugo. Armed agents in navy flak jackets with the big red CRS badge on their chest broke down the Mifubas front door with a battering ram and surged inside.

Neither the president nor his son was present. Mifuba Senior was in Kongolo. His son Fredy was in Paris but he had spent the night with his girlfriend at her penthouse on Île Saint-Louis.

The police went from room to room rousting the staff

of twelve who were taken by surprise. They were herded, many in their night clothes, into a downstairs room and not allowed to leave for several hours.

"Where are the keys to the cars?" shouted the Inspector in charge.

A frightened maid showed him up to the master bedroom. Hands shaking, she pulled open a drawer in a Chippendale dresser. The Inspector rummaged through a jumble of keys and electronic fobs bearing emblems of Rolls Royce, Bugatti and others. He scooped them up and took them outside where he thrust them at a sergeant.

"Here's a puzzle for you," he barked. "Match the keys to the vehicles. Then drive them all back to the station. They can stay in the police garage for now."

The sergeant grinned. He enlisted a couple of troopers and in the course of the morning they removed four expensive cars – a Bugatti, two Aston Martins and a Bentley – from their places by the kerb, as well as four others in the underground garage.

More agents searched the house. Computers and metal filing cabinets were taken away. The agents tried to be careful with the cabinets but the ornate plaster moulding around some of the doors got badly chipped.

The inspector called a locksmith who came and changed the locks on the front and back doors. That done, the inspector addressed the servants. "Who is the senior person here?"

A grey haired African stepped forward. "That would be me."

"What is your name?"

" Alphonse."

"Well, Alphonse, you and the others must pack up your stuff and leave. You have twelve hours."

"But . . ."

"Anyone not leaving will be arrested."

This set up a flurry of phone calls between the live-in servants and their families who lived off site.

Nobody wanted to call the President or his son, knowing that the messenger would reap a torrent of abuse or worse, but finally, a nervous Alphonse phoned Fredy.

The young man went ballistic. "What about my cars?"

With everything else, Alphonse had rather lost track. He went out to look.

Fredy kept nine cars in Paris. There was only room in the garage for four and the rest lived on the street. They included a Bentley, a Ferrari and a Bugatti Veyron, combined value four million euros.

All had been driven away by the agents except for the Ferrari, which Fredy had taken to visit his mistress.

When he heard the news he drove straight to Avenue Victor Hugo. He was in time to watch a line of dishevelled staff being hustled out of the house, carrying suitcases, trash bags and whatever else they could cram their belongings into. From his vantage point in the Ferrari he could see crime scene tape and uniformed agents blocking the doors.

He almost leaped out to protest but when he realised that the Ferrari would be a tempting target, he drove on.

One alert agent, busy unlocking a silver Rolls, spotted the Ferrari and tried to follow it but Fredy rounded the corner and was gone.

The anger engendered in the Mifubas, both father and son, by this exercise knew no bounds.

Fredy was down to his last car. True, a Ferrari was not chopped liver, but two days ago he had owned nine automobiles in Paris alone.

He was furious. It wasn't just the value of the items. Cars were replaceable and money was something he had plenty of. It wasn't even the inconvenience since Mifuba Senior seldom visited Paris and his son had the pick of Paris hotels to choose from.

No, it was the insult. And the publicity, because the press had a field day. Facts about the family, their ruthless rise to power and their inordinate spending were contrasted with the grinding poverty of the rest of Kongolo's population. Photos of cars similar to those impounded were displayed by the media to good effect.

Fredy was not completely surprised at the seizure. He had heard about the government's financial investigation, although he had paid little attention, considering it to be something for his father to worry about. But his reaction now was one of outrage. How could these nobodies disrupt his comfortable way of life, let alone steal his property?

His plans from now on would be inspired by one simple motive: revenge.

6

October 8th

Over drinks in the bar, Kathy confronted me again.

"We need to talk," she said.

"About?"

"You know, you and me."

"Oh, that."

"Yeah. I mean, you're not a bad guy, in fact, I almost like you."

"Why thanks."

"But you don't strike me as someone who is looking for a long term relationship."

I think I've mentioned that besides being good looking, Kathy is smart. It takes some women a while to figure out what she had just expressed in a second. But I wasn't over pleased with her observation, even if it were true. Truth is fine, but too much of it can be, well, too much.

"Define long term."

"In your case? Anything over a week."

"I plead guilty to that," I said, trying to sound amused.

"The thing about avoiding long term relationships is that you may end up not having any relationship at all," she said tartly.

One gift I do lack is the ability to tackle several problems at once. I felt like explaining that the issue with Zidane and terrorism was serious enough that I wasn't up to conducting a searching examination of my emotional life at the same time.

Kathy has a different kind of brain. She seems to be able to multi-task, keep going on several tracks without any loss of mental energy. If that worked for her, fine, but it doesn't for me. I changed the subject.

"Regarding Zidane's base in Paris, I'm thinking it must be somewhere low key," I said. "Not smart but not shabby either. We should make a list of areas and rank them according to what we think would be his criteria."

She seemed taken aback by this reasonable suggestion. It occurred to me later that her puzzlement may have been due to the rapid change of subject.

Fair enough, but there was work to be done.

September 24th

Zidane stared out of the window of his fourth floor walk-up flat in a nondescript part of the 14th.

He felt himself buzzing with unfulfilled energy. He sometimes wondered if there was something chemical in his brain that shouted, 'get out there and do something, make an impression on the world.'

He had achieved nothing lately. A year ago he had planted a small bomb on a bus in Marseille, but nobody was killed. He had been persuaded to use a bomb maker chosen by his customers, a radical Islamic splinter group. A faulty fuse had delayed the explosion and when it went off, rush hour was over and the bus was empty although the plan, obviously, was for it to be full. It reinforced

Zidane's belief that, to succeed, he must control all aspects of an operation.

That included finance. It was getting harder to raise funds. He had money of his own, carefully hidden, but it was his firm practice never to use it.

He walked down four dark flights of stairs – the building badly needed refurbishing – and bought a newspaper. He sat down at a sidewalk café nearby and ordered a hot chocolate.

He read about the raid on the Mifuba mansion with amusement.

His waiter also noticed the headline. He commented, "*Ça alors*, it's hard to feel sympathy for such rich people."

Zidane smiled politely.

"And all those cars, my goodness!" The waiter was a chatty soul and was not in the least discouraged by Zidane's lack of comment. "To live like that when people are starving in the slums, as we hear all the time, it's shocking, *n'est ce pas?*"

He finally looked at his silent customer and said, "Don't you agree m'sieu?"

Zidane smiled. "Oh yes."

That was the full extent of his comment, but the waiter deemed it enough. He removed Zidane's empty cup. The man was here most days. Not very sociable, a quiet one. He had never given him a second look.

Which was fine with Zidane. People didn't give him a second look because he was undistinguished; a man in his sixties, clean shaven, grey hair cut short, metal frames perched on his nose as he read. He could drink his choco-late in peace because there was nothing about him to attract attention.

He was turning the page when a thought made him pause, and he read the story again. One idea led to another. A plan started to form. Suddenly he felt cheerful.

He ordered another chocolate.

October 8th

Kathy had rented a small room on the 7th floor of the Meurice. Although Tisch was paying, she had told the clerk that she wanted their cheapest room. That had caused a double take from the man but resulted in a comfortable nook facing inwards onto the central well.

It reminded her of George Orwell's story in 'Down and Out in Paris and London' about the waiter delivering a roast chicken. The waiter tripped as he walked along the corridor and the chicken sailed down the shaft of a service lift onto a litter of broken bread, torn paper and so on. Hotel staff rescued the chicken, wiped it off and completed the delivery. Orwell did not name the hotel but

Kathy could never walk past a service lift without thinking of it.

As she prepared for bed she replayed her conversation with Oliver. The more she thought about it the more irritated she got.

She felt patronised. By changing the subject so abruptly he had as good as told her she was being irresponsible.

She had actually been trying to clear the air between them with a view to making their dialogue more productive. Give me a break, she thought.

Getting dressed next morning, she was still analyzing Steele in her mind. From talking to Mimi she already knew some things about his background that he had been in no hurry to tell her himself.

He had been a high flyer at Oxford, earning first class honours. He had excelled as a trainee accountant with a London firm and been made a partner.

But then things had gone badly wrong.

The Senior Partner had tricked him into signing a financial statement without reading it. The statement was fraudulent, concealing the Senior Partner's embezzlement – he turned out to be a compulsive gambler and went to prison for two years.

Oliver was left bankrupt and looking foolish. Only a lenient judge had saved him from doing hard time. He left London with his reputation in shreds, and bounced around Florida as a freelance financial investigator. It was a living, but a far cry from his former promise.

None of that showed in his manner. He was courteous and mildly patrician, with a BBC accent and a somewhat limited sense of humour. He was a decent athlete, having represented Oxford at squash, whatever that was. He was tolerable company although his attitude towards her seemed very reserved.

Still, if you had to work with a chauvinist pig the fact that he was a polite one was something at least.

She considered what to wear. As a traveller her choice was limited, but she had a couple of skirts that might fit the bill. She decided on the shorter of the two. Then she squeezed into the tightest of her tee shirts.

Arresting but not over the top she thought, looking in the mirror. Standards in Paris were high and she wanted to strike a transatlantic note without looking like a tart.

9

September 24th

Zidane let himself into his poorly lit apartment. He ought to have the windows cleaned but he hated to let anyone come to the flat. Nobody knew where he lived, and he wanted to keep things that way.

He stood in front of the mirror.

He might be inconspicuous but he was also vain. He would spend hours adjusting a lock of hair, changing his facial appearance using cheek pads or practising a modest smile, the one that let him get away with saying so little.

Sometimes he would talk to his reflection, his only confidant.

"Well, my friend, I may be onto something."

His reflection nodded. "A source of funds?"

"I think so."

"That would solve a few problems."

Zidane explained, "In return, I can offer something my source may want: a chance for revenge."

"Is he willing to pay for that?"

"He might be."

"What do you think he's worth?"

Zidane shrugged. "A lot."

He thought about the newspaper article.

There were photos of the mansion and one of the president himself, an official portrait taken some years ago. There was also a picture of his son Fredy leaving a nightclub with a young woman.

Pride of place was given to the expensive cars. The editors clearly understood the *schadenfreude* their readers would feel – quiet pleasure at the misfortunes of the rich.

He could well imagine the rage the Mifubas must be feeling against the French state. It was a rage Zidane shared, although for different reasons, and the bond that he felt with the president and his free-spending son was surely something that could be exploited.

He wondered how much money he would need. He had been thinking about the assassination of a leading public figure which was primarily a matter of meticulous planning. Funds were necessary, but not in massive amounts. He reflected ironically that tapping into the

Mifubas' money almost seemed a waste of a resource, if they had virtually unlimited wealth.

"Am I missing an opportunity somehow?" he asked his reflection.

"You don't have to spend money just because it's there, that's extravagant," was the pious reply.

But then came another thought. If money was no object, what could he plan that would really grab the headlines?

Something that would take the world by storm?

The answer startled even him.

10

October 8th

I n the Meurice bar, after Oliver and Kathy had left, Tisch looked at Kon Feaver. Kon looked back at Tisch.

"Why are you still here?" asked Tisch.

"I don't know. Because you invited me?"

"You must make a contribution," said Tisch. "Use your skills."

Kon smiled. "What skills?"

He was used to Tisch. Tisch and Kon's father Ari had been friends coming up in Goldman Sachs many years ago, but Ari Feaver had tired of Wall Street and moved to Israel where he had risen to become a governor of the

Bank of Israel. Kon had grown up as a son of privilege in Jerusalem and Tel Aviv.

But he had been an uneasy fit in the role. After that abbreviated spell in the Israeli Air Force, he kicked around the world as a mercenary in the Congo and a drug runner in Miami before settling down, relatively speaking, as a jack of all trades in the Florida Keys.

"I can fly a plane and sail a boat, but I don't see the need for either here."

Tisch nodded.

Neither of them mentioned Feaver's two other occupations.

One was being a nominee director in several of Tisch's racier companies, ones where Tisch didn't want to soil his own name, or put his own assets at risk. Feaver had no assets – even his boat was owned by a Panamanian corporation whose true ownership was untraceable – so he could go bankrupt without feeling any pain.

His other sideline was ferrying – don't call it smuggling – Cuban refugees from Cuba to Florida. He accepted only minimum payment for that because he thought the Castros and communism were absurd and he derived much satisfaction from a job well done when he got back home to Coquina Key. As a result, he had many Cuban-American friends and could rely on a slap-up Cuban meal whenever the urge struck.

"I'm thinking of the general scrambling ability that has kept you alive in some risky situations in the past," said Tisch.

"Couldn't have put it better myself," Kon agreed.

"Go away and think about what Steele and Kathy are doing and fit yourself in, any way you can."

Which proved not only that Tisch had a certain shrewdness, but that he knew his man.

11

September 24th

Zidane sat down at the computer. It was time for some research.

He was now thinking about a bomb rather than a shooting.

But what kind of bomb?

The breakthrough idea that had struck him was: if a bomb, why not nuclear?

It had taken a few days to get used to the idea, it was extreme, yet so obvious.

It soon became clear, as he searched, that detailed information was scarce. There were no manufacturing drawings of nuclear weapons on the Internet, although there was plenty of description of a journalistic kind.

He knew about the idea of 'critical mass' that was basic to all nuclear explosions – you had to have a piece of fissile material that was big enough. Below that size, the splitting of atoms would just fizzle out but above it, a compounding effect – the 'chain reaction' – occurred incredibly fast, resulting in the famous mushroom cloud.

There were *gun-type* bombs and there were *implosion* bombs. In the former, a hollow projectile made of fissile material was shot, as in a gun, onto a spike of the same material, thus completing the 'critical mass.'

In an *implosion* device, a spherical lump of plutonium was located at the centre of a much larger mass of uranium and, outside that, by layers of conventional explosive, like a bullseye. When the explosive was detonated it forced the uranium inwards, compressing the core and causing the necessary mass.

Two different techniques, both capable of causing the devastation seen in those chilling photos of Hiroshima and Nagasaki.

Zidane, with his engineer's brain, absorbed all this with ease. He noted wryly that, given a good machine shop he could almost have built the components himself. But not the fissile material. There was the problem. For that, you needed gas chromatographs and those were not something you could easily rig up in your garage.

. . .

There were also references to much smaller bombs. Suitcase bombs, they were sometimes called. He wondered if there were any of those already in existence and, if so, how he could get his hands on one?

The worldwide population of nuclear weapons had peaked during the Cold War at the mind-boggling number of 47,000. After that, various treaties and the breakup of the Soviet Union led to much moving around of weaponry.

For instance, 1,400 weapons remained in Kazakhstan after the Soviet break-up. Reportedly they were all returned to Russia and accounted for. He wondered about that. But he could not find any reports that would lead him to think he could acquire one.

He thought about the 'non-thermonuclear' countries.

Like Britain and France, India and Pakistan were esti- mated to have something of the order of 100 to 300 devices each. Such numbers were small compared to USA and Russia, which still had 5,000 to 10,000 each, and which, presumably, controlled them incredibly tightly.

He briefly considered Israel. Fat chance there, he thought, given his well known hatred of that state.

He was getting a headache. He closed the computer and went and made a cup of coffee. He could see how little he really knew about the whole subject. The idea of building a device himself was clearly not realistic.

No, he would have to rely on others to provide the

bomb. And that would take money, probably a lot of money.

How could he make contact with the Mifubas?

12

_____

October 10th

I went to see Tisch next morning.

The sun was shining after the rain the night before. Banks of flowers splashed daubs of colour in the Tuileries Gardens opposite the hotel. We went for a stroll.

"I've been trying to imagine what Zidane is planning to do with two million dollars," I said.

"And?"

"That's big money. It's far more than he would need to mount even a major campaign."

"Where does the money go, in something like that?" asked Tisch.

"Not being a terrorist I don't know."

"Take a guess."

"Weapons are expensive but not that expensive," I said. "Two million would buy a thousand automatic rifles. Travel is expensive too, but that kind of money would take a hundred terrorists round the world a few times, and that's flying first class."

"What about a really big bomb?"

I shook my head. I couldn't see it.

"Or several bombs."

"Nuclear?" I said tentatively.

"You're joking."

"Am I?"

A long pause.

Tisch looked grave. "Are you saying Zidane wants to set off a nuclear bomb?"

"I'm saying it's possible."

"And that Paris would be destroyed?" His voice rose slightly.

"Not necessarily."

"What do you mean, not necessarily?"

I tried to explain. "It would depend on the size of the weapon. It could be a suitcase bomb. Those are typically rated at about two kilotons of TNT, smaller than the Hiroshima bomb which was fifteen kilotons. So it could be about one sixth the size of Hiroshima."

I knew how grim that sounded, and the look he gave me only confirmed the impression.

"Do such bombs exist?"

"Very much so. The Russians designed something

called the PP1 which is shaped like an artillery shell – eighteen inches long and six inches in diameter. It is heavy – about a hundred pounds – but it would fit in a domestic suitcase."

"Not something you could carry in one hand unless you were a weightlifter," said Tisch.

"True. But the real value of such weapons is that, like a suitcase, they can be moved easily across borders. No need for tanks or rocket launchers. It's hard to defend against something like that."

"It sounds like science fiction."

"They are fact, not fiction, I'm afraid. Both Russia and the United States have developed even smaller devices, that would fit in a backpack."

"How powerful are those?"

"Only about a quarter of a kiloton. But if used in a crowded place – a monument , say, or at a busy intersection – the death toll would be staggering."

Tisch nodded. His air of anxiety had given way to his usual brisk manner. I was relieved. I knew him to be resilient but for a moment I feared he had lost his emotional equilibrium, something I had never seen happen before.

I should have known better, though. Carlton had been through a lot in life and it showed on his lined face, weathered as it was from sailing. It was unsmiling but not without humour – the humour of an entrepreneur who had seen ups and downs, fortunes made, lost and made again.

The hard times were behind him now. Eastern Debt Factors had been his final attempt after several failures. The timing had been perfect. It succeeded spectacularly and went public after a few years, making Carlton very wealthy. He was still EDF's biggest stockholder but he was also diversified to the point where his financial position was unassailable.

My own finances had improved since I met Carlton. I was paying down the bankruptcy debt I incurred when my former boss went to jail and nearly took me with him. I still owed almost a million dollars – the opposite end of the scale from Carlton.

Anyway, I could see he had collected himself. He had got a grip and would not waver again.

"Where does that leave us?" he asked.

"It means we must find this character soon, or something dreadful will happen."

13

September 25th

Zidane checked the Paris phone directory. There was a listing for Mifuba, somewhat to his surprise. He dialled the number. It rang twice but before it could be answered, he changed his mind and hung up. If the number was still active the police might be monitoring it. A face-to-face meeting would be much better.

It would require some preparation.

He left the apartment and caught the metro to Porte Dauphine. From there, he walked along Avenue Bugeaud and, turning onto Avenue Victor Hugo, approached the Mifuba mansion. A few metres away he sat down on a convenient bench, spreading a copy of Le Figaro in front of his face.

Nothing happened at first but he had trained himself to be patient.

After about an hour, an elderly man of African appearance approached. He passed close to Zidane, went up to the house and rang the bell. A blue-uniformed guard opened the door and came and stood on the step, machine gun slung over his shoulder.

It seemed that the visitor wanted to enter. The guard looked bored. He shook his head several times. Then he made a dismissive gesture, turned and went inside, slamming the door. The African turned and walked away.

Zidane followed him at a distance.

The old man walked to the end of the road and turned left into Rue des Belles-Feuilles. A few yards later he came to a small café with outside tables. Apparently on the spur of the moment, he stopped and sat down. Zidane sat down too, a couple of tables away. A waiter appeared and they both, separately, ordered coffee.

Zidane glanced over at the man who was staring into space, looking the picture of dejection.

Zidane got up and approached him. "*Vous permettez?*"

The old man looked up and shrugged. Zidane sat down.

"I was walking on Avenue Victor Hugo when I saw you having a discussion outside the big house with what looked like a policeman. I couldn't help wondering what was going on there?"

"And you are?"

"Oh, forgive me, I am a journalist. I work for Le Monde." He produced a card which he waved quickly in front of the man. "May I know your name?"

"Alphonse." He appeared to accept the ID uncritically. "If you are a journalist you probably know more than I do."

Zidane nodded. "Well, we know that the assets of the Mifuba family have been frozen as part of a Government investigation."

Alphonse frowned. "Yes, and that is all very well, but what about me and the other staff? We were expelled yesterday and I still have belongings in the house."

"Do you have anywhere to live?"

He nodded. "Most of us have relatives somewhere in Paris – I have a daughter and son-in-law in the Clichy-sous-Bois district. It's not a good area but it's a place to stay at least."

"Well, that is something."

"Nothing to compare with our leader!"

"You mean President Mifuba?"

He shrugged. "I wouldn't know about him. I mean his son."

"You don't care for him?"

Alphonse looked annoyed and also nervous. "This is off the record?"

"Of course."

"He should have made arrangements for us. He has done nothing."

"Is that typical?"

Alphonse was silent but his face betrayed a lack of affection for Fredy.

Zidane assumed a solicitous look. "Perhaps he too has a problem of where to live?"

Alphonse just shrugged.

Zidane pressed, "But then I suppose he can afford to stay in the best hotels."

"Doesn't need to, does he? Not with his girlfriend there!"

"Girlfriend?"

"Katerina Arnau. The model."

Zidane smiled. "I'm afraid I don't know much about models."

"Yes, a Brazilian girl."

"They are an item, as the expression goes?"

"It is common knowledge. It's nothing new, he changes his girlfriends with his underwear." The old man sniffed and spat on the sidewalk.

"Where does this model live?"

"She has an apartment on Île Saint-Louis."

Zidane sucked his teeth as if sharing the old man's disapproval. "Can I offer you a Calvados to go with that coffee?"

There was no dissent, so he beckoned the waiter and they sipped in silence.

"So the police took all those cars?"

"Except the Ferrari. Fredy was driving that and he was across town at the time. He'll just replace them. Easy come easy go." Alphonse's tongue was looser now.

"Ferrari, eh? One of my favourite cars."

Alphonse gave him a look.

"If I could afford one, of course," said Zidane. "What model is it?"

"Who knows? It's bright yellow."

He looked at his watch, appearing restless.

Zidane stood up. "Well, thank you, this has been really useful."

"When will your report appear?"

"Next week," said Zidane. "Don't worry, there will be nothing to suggest where I got my information." He put some money on the table and walked away.

He was going to need a car. He went by the Hertz office and rented a small Renault, nothing fancy, and half an hour later he was on the Île Saint-Louis. He cruised the streets of the small island until, with a jolt of excitement, he came upon a yellow Ferrari parked by the kerb. This must be Katerina's building. Once again he settled down to wait.

Half an hour later, Fredy emerged from the building and Zidane followed him.

For the rest of the day he tracked Fredy's movements, from store to restaurant and then to the Bois de Boulogne. Late in the afternoon, Fredy went into a house there and Zidane took the opportunity to drive as fast as he could back to the Île Saint-Louis.

14

Katerina let herself in and dropped several carrier bags on the parquet.

She had only spent a couple of thousand dollars that day, which for her was pocket change. As a model she had to keep up appearances. Many of her outer garments could only be worn once or twice in public, so her closets were crammed with dozens of almost-new skirts, dresses and blouses. Several times a year she gave bags of clothes to charity just to make room for more.

She heard movement in the living room. Fredy must be back. She was surprised, because she had not seen his car downstairs.

"What's up Fredy?"

There was no answer so she picked up her bags and carried them into the bedroom where she spent a few minutes unwrapping her purchases, then went into the bathroom and tidied her hair in front of the mirror.

Satisfied with her appearance, she walked into the airy living room. Afternoon sun shone in through the full length sliding windows that opened onto the balcony opposite Notre-Dame.

She almost had a fit. The man on the couch was not Fredy.

"Who the hell are you?"

He smiled. It was not a reassuring smile.

15

M oments later the door opened and in walked
Fredy.

He and Zidane looked at each other.

Fredy initially assumed Zidane was a friend of Katerina's, but she explained, "This man forced his way into the apartment."

Fredy shrugged. He was not as upset as Katerina expected him to be. It was not his apartment after all. But he wanted to stay on her good side and he realised a show of manliness might please her, so he frowned at Zidane.

"What do you mean by this?"

Zidane produced his modest smile. "You must be Mr. Mifuba? I'm delighted to make your acquaintance. May I say how shocked I was to read about the disgraceful behaviour of the French authorities."

Fredy nodded. Zidane had touched the right spot.

"What do you want?" blurted Katerina. She could see

the men beginning to establish a rapport and it made her resentful.

"Just a word with Mr. Mifuba."

"Go ahead then."

Zidane looked embarrassed. "It's a business matter." He paused.

Katerina walked over to the bar, opened the door of the small 'fridge and poured herself a glass of champagne from an open bottle in the door. She came back and sat down deliberately.

The two men exchanged looks. Clearly, she was not going to accommodate them by leaving.

Zidane nodded at Fredy. "You have a delightful balcony. Shall we go and admire the view?"

The men walked outside and Zidane carefully slid the glass door shut behind them.

Standing outside they looked down at the cathedral and, beyond, to a succession of ancient bridges over the grey river leading to distant outlines of the Louvre and the Eiffel Tower.

"A beautiful city," murmured Zidane.

Fredy grunted.

"But the government, that is not so beautiful, I think you would agree," Zidane went on.

He waited for Fredy to respond, but the African said nothing.

"You don't know me of course, but we have a common interest," Zidane prompted.

"Which is?"

"To express our views about their behaviour."

"I want to do more than that," said Fredy.

Zidane again waited for him to continue but he did not elaborate. Finally, Zidane said, "Perhaps you would like to do something that will make a major statement?"

"Damn right."

"I can help you."

Fredy strolled to the other end of the balcony and paused as if thinking, then came back and stood inches away, thrusting his face at Zidane. "Who are you?"

"My name is Omar Chadeau." It was a name he used on occasion.

"But who are you *really*? And why should I believe you when you make that kind of promise?"

Zidane paused for a long time. It was a moment of truth because it required him to share information that could cost him his life.

"I'll tell you on one condition," he said. "If, based on what I tell you, you are willing to work with me, will you provide me with finance of two million dollars?"

Despite how it might seem to outsiders, Fredy was not reckless with money. It was true that he spent lavishly on rich men's toys like the Rolls and the Bugatti, but he always knew where the money was coming from and he always paid cash. The fact that the cash was stolen from the people of Kongolo was another issue. He might be corrupt and a thief, but he was a good money manager. He only spent on things he wanted and, generally, he got good value for money.

So he paused, but only for a moment, then nodded. This was something he wanted. Two million was a lot, but they were only talking so far, and talk was cheap

Zidane tried to hide his elation. Asking Fredy to hand over two million dollars based on a verbal promise might have seemed reckless, but he had done his homework. Kongolo was only in the second tier of world oil producers but it produced half a million barrels of crude oil a day, worth about $30 million. Annually, that was ten billion dollars.

Sources estimated that eight billion of that went into the pockets of the president and his family, while the rest of Kongolo's one million citizens were starving or close to it.

Zidane himself lived comfortably on a lot less than $80,000 a year. The Mifubas' household income was 100,000 times that. So $2 million meant little more to Fredy than a twenty dollar bill meant to Zidane, he told himself.

He leaned forward. Even though they were alone on the balcony, he lowered his voice and spoke into Fredy's ear.

Fredy did not ask precisely how the money would be used. When he heard that a nuclear device was involved, he accepted that it would be expensive. Various people in the supply chain would have to be paid off. But if the bang was big enough it would be worth the money.

. . .

Zidane was not motivated by greed. But he was shrewd. Out of Fredy's $2 million, he planned to disburse $1.6 million but the other $400,000, he would unabashedly keep. It was his commission. Given the complexity and risk involved, he considered it reasonable.

He kept an account at the Vaduz, Liechtenstein branch of a private Swiss bank. The account was held by a Liechtenstein trust of which he was the sole trustee. Nobody knew of the account except his Liechtenstein attorney and even if someone learned about it and tried to track it down, the process would take years, so he knew that his funds were safe from prying eyes.

16

O n his way home Zidane was quietly pleased.

He did not have money in his pocket, nor even a firm promise from Fredy, but he knew he had his fish on the line. The way Fredy's eyes lit up when Zidane mentioned a massive explosion had been gratifying.

He spoke to his reflection in the mirror, "I think we have a live one, I really do."

"What motivates this guy?" asked his reflection.

"He's very bitter about the government confiscating his assets."

"Does he have justification?"

Zidane shrugged. "Does that matter?"

"It might."

"Well, no, he doesn't have much justification. The Mifubas have been raping Kongolo for decades, diverting the country's oil revenue to their own use. Now the French are cracking down, not because they sympathise with the Kongolese people but because the refinery went up in smoke and reduced France's oil supply."

"That might annoy me too," said his reflection.

"And me," said Zidane.

"When do you think he'll make up his mind?"

"I don't know. But I think I'll be hearing from him before the end of the week."

17

In fact, Fredy telephoned Zidane the same day.

He was intrigued by the Algerian's proposal, but he was also wary. He was a fair judge of character and there was something about the bland little man that made him uneasy. He did not let Zidane see it but he got the feeling that here was someone who could not be manipulated.

On the contrary, he guessed that Zidane was a manipulator himself, and would handle Fredy skilfully, given half a chance.

"I'm interested," he said. "But we need to meet one more time."

"Okay. How about Brasserie Lipp tomorrow, 12 noon?"

"Very well."

. . .

They sat opposite each other. Fredy studied the menu. He did not care for what he saw, being used to more refined fare, but he ordered cassoulet, the savoury concoction of pork sausage, goose, duck, mutton and white beans, stewed for hours at low temperature, for which Lipp was renowned. Zidane ordered bratwurst and sauerkraut.

"Well, what have you decided?" Zidane asked.

"I'll probably do it," said Fredy. "But I want to know something. How many deaths will be involved?"

"How many do you want?" asked Zidane, spearing a sausage.

"Thousands."

Their eyes met.

"So be it," said Zidane.

When it came time to leave, the two men, by agreement, headed for different Metro stations. Zidane walked to Rue du Bac and Fredy went to Saint-Germain-des-Prés.

But unknown to Zidane, a third person had been present at lunch, sitting alone on the far side of the room. She got up and followed Zidane. She got off at the same station and followed along behind him towards Rue du Parc-de-Montien.

Zidane never suspected that he was being followed. That was unlike him, careful as he was in such matters. But he was on something of a high as he strolled along, thinking about the encouraging way his plans were working out, and he dropped his guard.

He also would not have believed that gruff Fredy was subtle enough to take such action. He was in good company there. Not many people understood the level of cunning that was inbred in a family who had hacked their way to power in one of the richest but most primitive countries in Africa.

Katerina enjoyed the charade. It was all a bit of a game. Fredy had asked her to do this for him but he had not told her who Zidane was, so she had no idea of the danger she would face if she were spotted.

All she knew was that the mild little man was doing a business deal with Fredy and that, for some reason, he would not reveal where he lived. She was happy to help Fredy – he didn't often ask favours and it made her feel wanted.

She had given a lot of thought to her appearance, using her fashion knowledge to imitate a certain type, the sort of woman who would be comfortable lunching alone in a popular restaurant.

She wore a dark suit, good but not flashy, its design showing the influence of Coco Chanel. But she paired it with an unfashionable grey blouse that somehow skewed her appearance towards the everyday, rather than the elegance she was capable of displaying for an upmarket fashion show.

She chose one of her less stylish handbags and combed her hair to cover part of her face, but without making it seem that she was hiding. As a final touch, she painted her lips a shade too strongly and wore the reading glasses that she used at home but never, in her vanity, let the public see.

She ordered a salad and pecked at it while sending numerous text messages on her phone. She was the picture of an ambitious female executive preoccupied with her career.

Zidane had looked around the restaurant in a quick sweep from time to time but, to her credit, Katerina never caught his eye.

Following him afterwards, she walked straight past when he let himself into his building on Rue du Parc-de-Montien. A couple of blocks later she caught a taxi back to her flat, removing her lipstick in the back of the cab and heaving a sigh of relief.

18

Fredy was watching a game show on the big flat panel television. He looked at her enquiringly.

She gave him a thumbs up. "He lives on Rue du Parc-de-Montien!"

"Nice work."

She peeled off her jacket, then the plain blouse, and tossed them on a chair.

"Thank God I don't have to wear this dreadful outfit any more."

He eyed her appreciatively. The thin blue bra was decidedly un-dreadful.

"I don't understand what's happening," she said. "You must have something really important going on, to justify this cloak-and-dagger stuff."

"You could say so."

"Want to tell me?"

He shook his head. "It's a long story. Don't worry about it."

She felt a twinge of irritation. That was how he tended to treat her. It was the 'little woman' thing, which was not what she was. She was a successful, highly paid individual, one of the best in the world at what she did.

He saw that he might have gone too far, and quickly came over and put his arms around her, gripping her close.

Something about the drama of what was going on gave a special electricity to their embrace. He felt for the zipper at her hip and tugged it gently down. She wriggled out of her skirt and let it fall on the floor. Smiling tolerantly, she pulled him towards the bedroom.

Half an hour later, Fredy's mobile phone rang. He padded into the living room to answer it, leaving Katerina lazing in the big double bed. She could hear him talking. His comments were curt but she could tell that it was Zidane calling.

"I realise the location is critical," Fredy said.

Moments later, "The distance to Île Saint-Louis must be considered."

Apparently, there was agreement because then Fredy said, "And equally to Parc-de-Montien."

There was then a pause.

Finally, Fredy said, "Are you still there?"

The answer must have been affirmative because he

then said, "Good, we'll speak soon," and the conversation ended.

19

Zidane drew a sharp breath when Mifuba mentioned Parc-de-Montien.

He was furious. He had never mentioned his residence to Mifuba. Somewhere, he had made a mistake.

It told him two things. First, he had underestimated the African. The spoiled playboy was more intelligent, or at least more cunning, than he had thought.

Second, there was somebody else in the know.

He thought back, reviewing the time he and Fredy had spent together. It should not be hard to figure out where the problem lay. He searched his memory, from when he had glanced around the tables at Brasserie Lipp. He replayed the pictures in his mind and one came back more vividly than any other.

Of course! The professionally-dressed woman eating by herself and texting on her cell phone. He could see it now, as he analysed her appearance. There were a number of differences between her and Katerina, but the differences were not exclusionary, they could all be accounted for by dress, hairstyle and so on, superficial things. He himself had been too casual and he had been made to look a fool.

He hoped Mifuba had not noticed his involuntary hesitation on the phone.

How should he react? Adjust the program in some areas of detail and press on, of course.

The main adjustment would have to involve Katerina.

20

The Pakistani embassy is on Rue Lord Byron, a stone's throw from the Arc de Triomphe.

The phone rang in the second floor office of Cultural Attaché Munir Chaudry.

"Mr. Chaudry?"

"Yes?"

"My name is Omar Chadeau, sir. I am a professor of cultural anthropology at the University of Brazzaville in the Republic of Congo. I have a proposal that will greatly benefit your country's interests here in France."

Chaudry hesitated. "I see."

He didn't, but the proposition was so general that he could hardly reject it out of hand. And the Brazzaville reference was intriguing.

The caller said, "I hear the lunch buffet at Kashmir House is outstanding."

It was a smart move, to mention a good Indian restaurant. Chaudry looked at his watch.

"In half an hour?"

"Perfect," said the professor.

In the small restaurant on Rue de Chabrol, Chaudry raised his Cobra beer and nodded across the table at the man who called himself Chadeau.

"Cheers!"

Omar Chadeau smiled pleasantly. He was slim, white, about sixty, of medium height, grey hair starting to recede. Metal framed glasses perched on the bridge of his nose. A studious expression that made it easy to accept his self-description as a professor at a Central African university.

"I wasn't sure how you would feel about a Kashmiri restaurant, given the dispute between India and Pakistan, but the food here is excellent."

Chaudry smiled. "There's a detente when it comes to good cuisine."

They exchanged small talk as they addressed a searingly hot lamb vindaloo, accompanied by spiced eggplant and pureed lentils.

Finally, Chaudry said, "You have good taste."

"Thank you."

"Now, please explain why we are here."

"Of course. To put it briefly, I am in a position to direct a large sum of money to appropriate Pakistani causes."

"How much?"

"Seven figures."

"For what causes?"

"Scientific and technical knowhow."

"Can you be more specific?"

"The use of nuclear power."

There was a pause before Chaudry replied.

"I'm a cultural attaché. My area of interest is not technical. Why are you approaching me, rather than one of my colleagues?"

Chadeau nodded. Although there was nobody within earshot, he leaned forward and lowered his voice.

Zidane, alias Chadeau, had no idea, when he first approached Chaudry, how his overture would be received. Everything would depend on the man's amenability to a very unorthodox proposition. He had been fully prepared to halt the conversation at the first sign of a problem and start again somewhere else.

But Chaudry turned out to be a good choice. By the end of the luncheon, two things had been established.

First: the nuclear power to which Chadeau referred was not necessarily limited to peaceful use.

Second: the funds in question would not be routed to a government agency. Instead, they would flow initially into the hands of Munir Chaudry himself.

21

October 9th

My phone rang. It was Kathy.

"You'd better get round here."

"What's going on?"

"Saadi is dead."

Carlton had the Presidential suite on the ground floor. It was expensively decorated with chandeliers and heavy silk curtains, but I hardly noticed them, magnificent though they were.

Carlton, Mimi and Kathy were all there.

"What happened?" I asked Kathy.

"He fell in front of a subway train just after leaving us.

His office just got a call from the police. They identified him from his driver's license."

I was shaken. Saadi had seemed pleasant, and engagingly modest about his skills. I had been looking forward to working with him.

"We wondered if he had a dizzy spell," said Mimi. "He didn't look too robust."

I scoffed at that. "Try something more sinister."

"Why?"

"The circumstances. The fact that he came to see us. Somebody didn't want him to talk. They were too late to stop him from speaking to us, but at least they could prevent further damage by silencing him afterwards."

"I've spoken to his employer," said Tisch. "We can go round there, he's expecting us."

We took a taxi to Goldhawk Investments, on Avenue Montaigne. The street is smart, full of couturiers and high end retailers. Goldhawk's lobby was decorated entirely in gold, a play on its owner's name.

We were shown to a fourth floor office overlooking the street. The gold motif was continued in the wallpaper. It was a bit overpowering.

A short, bald man greeted Tisch with a gruff, "Hi."

"Morning, Goldhawk." Tisch was equally terse. He sat down, uninvited, then remembered us. "This is my wife Mimi. And these are Kathy Smith and Oliver Steele, who help me out."

Solly Goldhawk, thirty pounds overweight, stuck out a hand without meeting my eye. He had a bright red face below a bald head, and a hooked nose like a parrot's beak. Full lips made him look rather feminine. From his colouring I suspected high blood pressure.

"A nasty business," said Tisch.

"Certainly is," said Goldhawk. "Saadi was irreplaceable." He sounded upset, but whether for business or personal reasons was unclear.

"What do we know?" I asked.

He noticed me for the first time. "It was rush hour. There were dozens of people on the platform, but nobody saw anything until after it happened."

"So he could have fainted?" asked Mimi.

"Or been pushed," I said.

"Either one," said Goldhawk. "A body toppling into space, who knows?"

"Has anyone contacted his family?" asked Mimi.

Goldhawk waved a hand. "It's being taken care of. They'll be looked after." He didn't sound broken hearted.

Carlton asked, "How can we build on what he was doing? Did he leave any notes?"

Goldhawk shrugged. "It's possible. He had assistants. They are on the second floor."

"Let's take a look," I said.

We trooped downstairs where the décor was less elegant – grey walls and frosted glass doors. Goldhawk selected an office and strode in imperiously but, once inside, he seemed nonplussed. I got the impression that he seldom set foot there.

Two studious looking young men were sitting in front of computer screens. One of them, engrossed, continued typing but the other stood up and smiled.

"Pierre, this is Mister . . ." Goldhawk frowned at me. "What was your name?"

"Oliver Steele."

"Show Mr. Steele what Saadi was working on."

"Sorry for the sad turn of events," I said.

Pierre nodded appreciation. "I don't know if I can help," he said in accented English. "Saadi made very few notes, he kept a lot in his head. I do know that he was writing a program that would help him view aspects of the metadata."

He paused and looked at Goldhawk.

"That's all right," said Goldhawk. "You can speak freely."

Pierre smiled. "Some of what we do here is pushing the envelope in terms of legality."

"I was a tax accountant," I said. "I know about being aggressive in the grey areas."

He looked relieved. "Some of the data we work on is stuff we should not have access to at all. Saadi had found ways of downloading it."

"Yes, he explained that."

"He was also able to mimic the programs that government agencies themselves use to analyse data."

"So he was hacking into banks to get data and then hacking into the government to get the programs they use to analyse it?"

Pierre nodded.

"Sounds like a parallel operation to the French government's own espionage."

"Which the government denies exists," Goldhawk interrupted.

"Of course."

Goldhawk looked pretty pleased with himself and I could see why. It was a remarkable resource. He had set it up for commercial reasons but its power went well beyond that.

"We need some specific information," I said to Pierre. "It's really important. Can you log on to his computer for us, so that we can continue where he left off?"

He smiled apologetically. "I regret, but no."

"Why not?"

"We are just the supporting cast. We were carrying out tasks given us by Saadi. Neither Henri" – he indicated his colleague – "nor I have the skills to do the sort of thing he was doing. We don't even know what password he was using. There was a reason for that. The material is so sensitive that the fewer people who can access it, the better."

"But now we're stuck," I said.

Goldhawk looked annoyed. Clearly he was not used to being thwarted.

"Passwords can be broken, can't they?"

"They can but it takes time and I don't know how much

time we have," I said. "If somebody out there is planning to do something dreadful, we need to act fast."

Kathy said "Halfshaft."

Everyone looked at her.

"What shaft? said Goldhawk.

"Halfshaft. It's a person."

'Is that a bad guy?"

"No. He's the password king."

"What's she talking about," asked Goldhawk rudely.

I was getting a bit tired of Goldhawk. He was gruff like Carlton Tisch, but marriage to Mimi had rubbed some of the rough edges off Tisch, who was now almost tolerable. Goldhawk lacked polish.

"She's talking about Ron Halfshaft," I said. "He's a programmer. We've used him before."

Kathy had hit on a good idea. I recalled a tense scene some time ago when Flack, Halfshaft's then-employer and a nasty piece of work if ever there was one, held a casino owner at gunpoint on Antigua while Halfshaft sat cracking the password to his programs so that Flack could steal them.

"He sounds British," said Goldhawk. "Get him here. He can take Eurostar. Tell him he can ride first class."

"He's American. He lives in Los Angeles," I said.

"Oh. Get him here anyway."

"I'll give him a call," I said.

There was a pause. After a minute I realised everyone was looking at me.

"Is there a problem?" I asked.

"No. Why aren't you calling him?" asked Carlton.

"I don't have his number at my fingertips," I said, irritated.

"So get it," said Goldhawk.

I love these capitalists, self-made and pushy, it seems to go together.

22

A s we were leaving, Solly Goldhawk drew me aside.

"You seem like a bright young man. What are you doing working for a bum like Tisch? You should come and work for me."

"I thought you and Carlton were friends."

"We are."

"Do you often poach talent from your friends?"

"All the time."

"You might think again if you knew my background," I said. I explained about being bankrupt.

I thought he would disapprove but he just laughed. "I went bankrupt twice before I was thirty. It was good for me."

"How so?"

"It helped me think clearly. When you've lost every-thing a couple of times it's much easier to take a punt on something that may really pay off. You have to be willing to do that."

"I also narrowly escaped going to prison."

"That sounds interesting,"

I explained that I had signed a phoney audit report that my boss Charlie Southampton had put in front of me late one Friday saying it had to catch the mail.

Goldhawk nodded. "The old 'it's very urgent' trick. I use it a lot. And you fell for it?"

"I was trying to seduce his daughter Serena at the time and I didn't want to piss the father off."

"And did you?"

"Piss him off?"

"No, seduce her."

"Afraid not. She was so cross about her dad going to prison thanks partly to my evidence that she went right off me."

Solly Goldhawk shook his head. "Shouldn't mix women and business. It never works."

"I guess you're right."

"So will you come and be my Vice-President for New Businesses?"

I smiled and shook my head.

But it was good for my ego.

23

October 6th

Zidane was having breakfast in his flat when the phone rang.

It was Munir Chaudry. The Pakistani spoke fast, almost gabbling.

"We should talk, and not on the phone."

Zidane mentioned a café on Boulevard Saint-Michel, not far from the Tour Montparnasse, the big skyscraper that dominated the skyline south of the river.

They sat outside, facing the wrought iron gates of the Luxembourg Gardens. There was a light breeze and Zidane reflected how delightful Paris could be in spring weather. He ordered a croque monsieur and Chaudry ordered coffee.

Chaudry was clearly excited. "Well, I've identified a source and the goods are ordered."

Zidane felt a surge of adrenaline. It was weeks sooner than he had expected. "Are you confident in your engineers?"

"They are the very best," said Chaudry with a hint of pride.

A pretty girl in a thin dress walked by and they paused to watch her progress.

"How do you want the product shipped?" Chaudry asked.

"It must be split into two parts so that neither half will look too much like a bomb. Each part will be transported separately."

"Should they go by sea? I was thinking Marseille. Security is very tight since Charlie Hebdo."

"Yes, it is. They'll be coming via Italy and Switzerland."

Chaudry was surprised. "But you will still have to cross borders to bring the product into France."

"Not true. Italy, France and Switzerland are all in the Schengen Zone."

"Meaning?"

"There is no border control between Schengen Treaty members. I can drive straight into France from Switzerland or Italy without being subject to inspection."

"Sounds too good to be true."

"It does, doesn't it?"

There was a brief silence of the kind that happens when good news is sinking in.

Zidane went on, "The heavier component will be shipped to Naples."

"Any special reason for that?"

He asks a lot of questions, thought Zidane. But Chaudry was useful for now, so he just nodded. "Naples is a big port. It's convenient. I have arranged with a freight forwarding company there to take delivery. Your engineer will send them the bill of lading."

"What about Customs?"

Zidane smiled. "I've anticipated that. As you know, the device is designed to fit in a suitcase. What do you think is the best way to conceal a suitcase?"

"I don't know."

"Why, in a consignment of suitcases, of course."

Chaudry was not sure whether Zidane was being facetious. But the Algerian reached in his pocket and produced a business card. "Let me introduce myself."

Chaudry studied the card, with a grainy finish suggesting leather.

'*Mario Perez, Sales Director*
Bagagli di Italia, Milano.
Luggage for people of taste.'

"Is that the name of a real corporation?" asked Chaudry.

"Of course. It has a legitimate street address too – only

a mailbox, but the paperwork makes it look like a real office."

"Very good."

Zidane nodded. "The shipment will consist of two dozen identical suitcases."

"I don't understand. Must I buy a bunch of suitcases?"

"No, that has been taken care of. The suitcases will come from China. They will arrive in Lahore in good time. Our particular suitcase will be inconspicuous because its weight will be averaged, so to speak, among the other cases."

"What about the other parts of the device?"

"The electronic section, the trigger and timing mechanism, will be airfreighted to Romanshorn."

"Romanshorn?"

"It's a small town in the German speaking part of Switzerland. There's nothing distinctive about Romanshorn, that's why I chose it."

"Fair enough."

"The goods will be described on shipping documents as 'horological equipment.'"

Chaudry laughed. "You've thought of everything."

Zidane tried not to feel irritated, but the suggestion that he would make any plan without thinking annoyed him.

"I hope so."

"I'm curious. When you pick up the main cargo, what will you do with all those empty suitcases?"

Chaudry was nervous, talking too much. Zidane stood

up and threw some money on the table. "No more questions."

"Of course. I'm sorry."

24

October 10th

The programmer Ron Halfshaft was on his way to Las Vegas when he got the call.

He was driving through the High Desert in a yellow Mustang with the black convertible top down. He had refuelled at Barstow and expected to reach Vegas in a couple of hours.

The Eagles were blasting away:

"On a dark desert highway, cool wind in my hair . . . "

He knew the words and sang along tunelessly.

He made this trip every month, travelling mid-week when hotel prices were lower. He would check into a good hotel on the Strip, head for the blackjack tables and start to win.

He had 'eidetic memory,' the ability to recall scenes visually in full detail, so he remembered what cards had fallen and could better predict which would be dealt next.

Counting cards was not illegal but it was very unpopular with casino management. If counters were caught they were warned off, politely but firmly. That never happened to Ron because he was not greedy. He didn't gamble for the money, but for pleasure in taking on the system and proving that he could beat it.

When he had a strong winning streak, he would follow up with an intentional losing streak, then get up and leave with a wry smile and some crack along the lines of, "Time to quit," or, "That's my limit, let's hope for better luck tomorrow." He would then move to another resort.

So he was never flagged and continued to win enough to cover room and board, going home with the satisfaction of knowing he had beaten the system.

"Mirrors on the ceiling,
The pink champagne on ice . . ."

The mobile phone rang, its signal over-riding the music.

"Yeah?"

"Ron?

"Yeah!"

"Oliver Steele."

"Oh, hi!"

Halfshaft knew exactly who was calling. Two years ago, he had worked for the Flacks, a dubious gambling outfit. They had been involved in the takeover of Casino Caribbean, an internet gaming operation on Antigua. Halfshaft had hacked into the casino's system and stolen the codes that enabled it to trade. He had last seen Oliver disappearing into the night on a high powered motor launch heading for the Florida Keys.

Later, he got bored, quit and returned to California.

Now he was back where he felt most at home, on the West Coast, with an apartment by the beach, surfboard in the garage, regular trips to Vegas – what more did a man need?

So when Oliver said, "I have a project that might interest you," his first question was, "Where?"

"Paris."

"Paris, France?"

"Where else?"

"What kind of project?"

Oliver explained. Halfshaft quite liked what he heard. "I'm pretty busy. I could maybe get to you in a couple of weeks."

"Ah," said Oliver. "The thing is, we need you now." He could have mentioned Saadi and the terrorist connection but he didn't want to complicate the story. In data processing, people understood that *now* meant *now*.

Halfshaft was not convinced. "See, I'm on my way to Vegas."

Oliver understood immediately.

"Where exactly?"

"Just past Barstow."

"In the Mustang?"

"Yeah."

Oliver thought for a moment. "You can gamble here," he said.

"In Paris?"

"Of course."

"I never heard they had casinos," suspiciously.

"Sure they do."

"Name one."

"Casino de France," Oliver guessed quickly. "It's world famous."

It was just enough. Halfshaft made a reluctant U-turn.

"Relax, said the night man,
We are programmed to receive.
You can check-out any time you like,
But you can never leave!"

He drove back past Barstow again and down from the desert, through San Bernardino and the heavily Chinese cities of San Gabriel and Monterey Park, to his flat in Hermosa Beach.

It was evening when he got home. He had picked up Mexican food on the way, it might be his last chance at Mexican for a while.

He watched the news on the seventy-two inch TV

screen that dominated his living room, munching carnitas tacos with guacamole.

Then he strolled down to the beach. He checked out the full moon reflected in the Pacific and took in several deep breaths of seaside air. Tomorrow it would all be a long way away.

Twenty-four hours later, Oliver met him off an Air France Jumbo at Charles de Gaulle.

25

A t the airport I ushered Halfshaft into a Peugeot taxi.

It was a fine morning which was just as well because he arrived wearing only jeans, alligator-skin boots and a cotton tee shirt emblazoned with the cryptic question, "Is there Life East of Sepulveda?"

On the way into town Ron stared out of the cab at the grey houses with their steeply raked roofs. On a blank wall he saw the sign:

"Défense d'Afficher, Loi du 29 Juillet, 1881."

"No bill posting? Sounds like a good idea."

"I didn't realize you spoke French." I knew he had never set foot outside the English speaking world.

"I don't, but I can read it."

"Well?"

"Well enough. I did some work for a French bank that was setting up in L.A. Their programmers didn't speak English too good, so I bought a French phrase book."

I winced at 'too good.' Lousy grammar from a smart guy.

Ron's eidetic memory is a gift that only occurs in a tiny number of people. It's not always accompanied by great intelligence although Ron has excellent programming skills. Its nature is something of a mystery. Some say it involves twisted synapses, the nerve strands that connect different areas of the brain.

"There's more to a language than learning a few phrases," I said.

"Yeah, but the book included declension of regular and irregular verbs in all tenses and the subjunctive, as well as rules and exceptions for gender of nouns – that kind of stuff."

Like many Britishers I speak schoolroom French and, like them, I try and make it go a long way. I live in the present, not using past and future tenses because I can't remember them. But this poorly dressed Californian had the lot at his fingertips after reading one thin book.

At Avenue Montaigne, I introduced Halfshaft to Pierre and Henri, who shook hands politely while staring at the alligator boots. I wondered if they would be able to work together, but my doubts were dispelled as soon as he sat down at Saadi's computer and started working the keys.

"We don't have Saadi's password," Pierre explained.

Halfshaft shook his head. "I use my own program. Shouldn't take more than ten minutes."

"Did you bring it with you?" I asked.

"Didn't need to." He proceeded to connect via the internet to a computer back in his Hermosa Beach flat.

"See, I flag the files I need and e-mail them to myself here in Paris."

The transfer only took a few moments. Then, Halfshaft initiated a routine that, as he explained, would spin through millions of possible combinations, trying each in turn.

"It's no big deal," he said. "It's as if you kept turning the tumblers on your padlock on your locker at the gym. Sooner or later you would hit the right combination."

In five minutes, the screen stopped flickering and came to rest, displaying the word, 'Fatima.'

"It's his wife's name," said Pierre.

"I'm surprised you guys didn't guess that," said Halfshaft.

So much for security, I thought.

"What are you looking for?" he asked.

I explained our need to know who Zidane had been talking to. Within minutes, he showed us a list of dozens of phone numbers, sorted with the most frequently called at the top.

"Is that it?" he asked.

I nodded. "But we need to know who they belong to."

"For that, you need a phone directory."

"There's one on the bookshelf," I pointed out.

"Electronic," he said, clearly amused at my naiveté.

Pierre understood. Leaning over Halfshaft's shoulder he navigated to the website of the French telephone system.

Things then got pretty confusing, at least for me. I tried to follow along but, with Halfshaft typing computer code on the fly, all I could do was sit and wait for him to finish.

Finally, by comparing two databases, he produced a list of ten names, with addresses also shown.

"Who are all these people?" I asked.

Halfshaft shrugged. "No idea."

There were also several numbers with no name listed.

"What are those?" I asked.

"Ex-directory."

"Okay."

"I can probably do something with them," he added.

At that point, I realised that I was going to need a different kind of help. I called Kathy.

"How goes the research?" she asked.

"I think we have some walking around to do."

I folded the list in two and gave half to Kathy. We then separated and set out in opposite directions.

I actually did my 'walking around' by taxi, but it certainly enhanced my knowledge of Paris streets.

The most frequently called number on my list was a corporation, *Compagnie Economique SARL*. near Parc-de-

Montien. The name offered no clues but when I got there it was a Chinese restaurant.

So now I knew what Zidane liked for supper. But it probably also told me the general area where he lived, assuming that he preferred not to drive too far for his Kung Pao Chicken. I made a note and drove to the next address.

The subscriber's name was Katerina Arnau. She lived on the Île Saint-Louis. I could tell the area was expensive just from the clean and well-kept exteriors of the houses. I got down a couple of blocks away and strolled back.

I was trying to be inconspicuous. It wasn't hard. Parisians march with a sense of purpose, showing little interest in those around them, whereas tourists, who seem to outnumber the natives, drift aimlessly, enjoying the sights. Either way, nobody seemed interested in me as I studied the brass-framed directory by the front door.

Katerina Arnau's apartment was on the sixth floor. When I stepped back and looked up I could see a long balcony, probably enjoying a fine view of the Seine. A sleek yellow Ferrari was parked nearby, blatantly defying a *Stationnement Interdit* sign. Several parking tickets adorned the windscreen.

I could have rung the doorbell – I was already dreaming up excuses to introduce myself to Ms. Arnau – but I decided not to. There was too much at stake for 'bull in a china shop' tactics. But I had the strong feeling that I was onto something.

It was getting late and rush-hour traffic was building.

My next address was across town so I decided to call a time-out. I phoned Kathy.

"Want to get together and compare notes?"

"Sure."

She was wearing low rider jeans and those pink sneakers. She had ditched the Miami Heat T-shirt and was wearing the Los Angeles Lakers equivalent which made me wonder about her capacity for loyalty.

"Any luck?" I asked.

"Maybe."

She smiled, as though she had seen something she liked.

"What does 'maybe' mean?"

"After a few dead ends I ended up getting the name of a cultural attaché at the Pakistani Embassy."

It struck me, not for the first time, that Kathy can be quite effective. It's probably why she gets on well with Tisch.

She also tends to have these offbeat ideas that add unexpectedness to her thinking. I find them a turn-on. The world likes to pigeonhole good-looking blondes as not too bright, so when one turns out to be smarter than me it's a kick.

While I was thinking about that she gave me a big wink as if she had read my mind and was agreeing.

26

Kathy explained. She had gone to the first address on her list, an apartment on Boulevard de Montmorency, a decent residential street in the 16th Arrondissement.

The apartment was on the third floor. The tenant's name was Munir Chaudry.

The door to the building was open so she walked straight in. On the right as she entered were the concierge's rooms.

"Hi!" She smiled and waved her scrap of paper.

The concierge, a skinny woman in her sixties with dyed red hair and an unfriendly expression unleashed a stream of French, probably thought Kathy, along the lines of, 'Who are you and what do you want?'

Sometimes in life, though not often, good luck strikes and it did so just then in the shape of a young man who walked into the building and paused next to them. Aged about thirty, in a grey suit and silk tie, he could have been a salesman or middle manager.

He acknowledged the concierge, nodded at Kathy and uttered the magic words in English, "Can I help?"

"I'm here to see Munir."

"I think he's overseas at the moment."

"Overseas?"

"In Pakistan."

She thought fast. "Again?" Artful, implying acquaintance without actually lying.

"Yes. That's diplomatic life, I guess."

"I guess so."

There was a brief silence. The concierge and the young man seemed to be waiting for Kathy.

"My brother and Munir play tennis together. I was in the area so I thought I'd stop by and say hello."

It was just babble. She could tell that her presence seemed slightly unusual but when in doubt, smile and keep talking.

The Frenchman nodded. A card appeared. "Well if I can be of further assistance, I should be honoured. Feel free to call." He bowed.

She studied the card. "Thank you, Mr. Dutrieux."

He smiled and bent his head. "Enchanté!"

Sometimes being blonde and pretty earned you the benefit of the doubt. She made an excuse and left.

So Chaudry was a diplomat, presumably with the Pakistan embassy. It was slight progress but a lot better than nothing.

27

So we've got a couple of leads worth following," I said.

Kathy nodded. "The Pakistani for one. Who's the other?"

I mentioned Katerina Arnau on Île Saint-Louis.

"Wow," she said.

"Wow?"

"You know who that is, don't you?"

"Should I?"

"She's said to be the highest paid fashion model in the world."

"French?"

"Brazilian."

"Well that's nice."

"How do we follow up?" she asked.

"I'll take the fashion model," I said.

"I thought you might."

I went back to Île Saint-Louis. The yellow Ferrari was still there. I rang the bell.

Just as I did so the door flew open and a man emerged. He was well dressed, self-important looking and African, apparently living in the same building as Katerina Arnau. He paused – I was standing directly in his way – and frowned.

"Bonjour," I said.

"What do you want?"

He spoke in English so either my Britishness was showing or he didn't speak French.

"Can I have a word?"

He stared at me. "Damn journalists."

"I'm not a journalist."

He shoved straight past me, his shoulder bumping mine. The impact nearly knocked me over. He was solidly built, several inches shorter than me but twenty pounds heavier. By the time I recovered my balance he had unlocked the Ferrari and was climbing into it. I considered yanking him out and punching him on the nose, but only briefly. Not the best idea.

He started the car. Time was short. I tried frantically to think of something that would make him stop and talk to me.

"What about Zidane," I shouted. Pretty crude.

Luckily the words were drowned out by the Ferrari's angry roar as it shot away from the kerb. I stood and watched as it rounded the corner, sped across Pont Louis Philippe and vanished into Paris traffic.

I went back and rang the bell of the Arnau apartment. I kept trying, but there was no reply.

28

Carlton's way with money takes some getting used to.

That's putting it mildly. If he wants to eat out he doesn't pop into the local bistro, it's *Le Grand Véfour* or nothing. So that was where our evening strategy session took place.

"What's new?" asked the skinny financier when we were all seated and sipping our drinks – beer for Carlton, some kind of rum drink with a little paper parasol for Kathy and a *Mojito* for me.

He listened to our reports.

"So we think Zidane lives in the 14th *arrondissement* and likes Chinese food. His chums include a Pakistani diplomat and a Brazilian model," he said when we finished speaking.

"That's about it."

"Not much to go on, is it?"

I bridled at that. He hadn't spent the day grinding around Paris.

"It's more than we had this morning," I said.

"The social level is surprising," said Kathy.

I wasn't sure what she meant.

"Well, apart from the Chinese restaurant, the contacts we found are respectable or even affluent individuals. "

"So?"

"Not typical associates for a terrorist bent on destroying society."

"Does that tell us anything?"

"Maybe not." She smiled. "But it's a jigsaw. The pieces will all join up in the end."

Carlton sniffed. I suspected he was in my camp and preferred logical connections. Jigsaws were for women.

"Keep looking," he said. "Maybe your friend Halfshaft will help with the 'ex-directory' numbers."

He turned to the menu. He ordered *Foie gras* followed by *Homard rôti dans sa carapace*. We joined in the spirit of things – nobody wants to watch a man eat alone. When the bill came, it roughly equaled a month's wage for the average worker.

I got to Avenue Montaigne at eight next morning only to find Halfshaft already there.

He was hammering away at the keyboard. Empty soda cans and congealed pizza told the story.

"He's been there all night," said Pierre.

"I'm nearly there. You just can't automate some stuff," said Halfshaft.

The printer hummed and spat out more names.

Kathy grabbed the paper. Every name was that of a bank. A couple were well known but I had never heard of the rest.

"How do we use this?" I asked.

"Same as before," said Kathy cheerfully. "We walk in."

"It's not that easy," I said. "Are you going to just march in and demand account information? They'll laugh at you."

She shrugged. "It was a thought."

"Let's meet again this afternoon," said Carlton. "Tea at the Meurice?"

I spent the day following up some other names but without much luck, apart from identifying Zidane's dry cleaner and the reservations office of Air France. By four o'clock I was ready for a break.

Carlton was sitting in the *le Dali* room beneath its spectacular Ara Starck ceiling, a refreshing contrast to the gilded opulence of the lobby.

He was scribbling in the margin of his International New York Times, the International Herald Tribune that was. There were boxes and arrows and scratchings out.

"Doing a spot of tax planning," he said.

His master company Eastern Debt Factors, an industrial scale moneylender, had operations in France and Germany run by capable executives whose management strategy was to keep Carlton from interfering at all costs.

"Is it panning out?"

"No, but it should. All the internet companies are doing it."

"How does it work?"

"You set up two subsidiaries in the Irish Republic and arrange transfer pricing and management fees so that the profit flows into a non-tax jurisdiction. It's called a 'Double Irish.' But I keep getting taxable income. Those West Coast kids play a load of monkey tricks."

So when the internet kids did it, it was monkey tricks but if used by Carlton, it was tax planning.

"Can I see?" I added a third little box and linked it with some dotted lines. "Try that."

"What's that box?"

"It's a Netherlands corporation."

Grudgingly, "Might work."

"It does. It's a double Irish with a Dutch sandwich. Have your accountants check it out. Who do you use?"

"LevyTeagardenHooper."

"The people with the funny name."

"They're the best," defensively.

"The biggest anyway," I said.

I don't often win a battle of wits with Carlton so it's sweet when I do. I was relishing my success when in walked Kathy, looking pleased.

"I'll have a pot of Lapsang Souchong and some cucumber sandwiches with the crusts cut off."

"Oui, Madame." If the waiter was upset at the idea that any sandwich could be served at the Meurice without being separated from its crust, he hid it well.

"Find anything useful?" I asked.

She produced a carrier bag full of what looked like annual reports. "Here are a few banks our friend had dealings with."

"You suppose."

She tossed her head back, brushing blonde hair out of her eyes. "I suppose." She tipped the colourful leaflets onto the table. "Banque National de Paris; Bank of Dubai; CBA – that's the Consolidated Bank of Africa."

"So?"

"She may have a point," said Carlton.

"Oh really?"

"It's consistent with his obtaining a large sum of money and sending it to a tax haven."

"Maybe."

"CBA is a Nigerian bank," said Carlton.

"It has branches in fifteen countries," said Kathy.

Carlton looked at her, impressed.

So she had read the brochure. Big deal. But I could see which way the wind was blowing. Carlton's attitude to young women is that the younger they are the more the old goat likes them. He's not exactly critical.

Kathy was his favourite, so I adopted an appreciative tone of voice, "That's certainly something to think about. If only we could set eyes on this fellow."

29

K athy wanted to concentrate, so she went and sat on a bench on the Avenue des Champs-Élysées and watched the people go by.

Actually, the traffic noise was deafening making it hard to focus on the people, but the trees were green and the general atmosphere conducive to reflection.

She thought about Oliver's experience at the Arnau residence. She guessed that the African was probably Fredy Mifuba. She read the popular press even if Oliver didn't and Fredy's affair with Katerina was widely reported.

She didn't know a lot about Mifuba but she did know that he was enrolled at Pepperdine, an expensive private university in Malibu, across town from her own *alma mater*, the University of Southern California. In fact, they had been contemporaries when she was studying for her Masters at USC.

The question was how to come face to face with him. She had never met him before, but she knew someone who had.

Princess Ranaraunaa of Ruonga, known to her friends as Rosie, was a classmate of Kathy's. They were of similar age although from different backgrounds. She and Kathy had met in the library at USC. In casual chat they discovered that they shared a dry sense of humour and a taste for barbecue and they had become friends.

Rosie was the daughter of the King of Ruonga, a Central African nation adjacent to Kongolo. She had an IQ of 170. Educated in England, she had graduated from Cambridge. With a model's slim figure and a smile to melt icebergs, she was quite the package.

There must be some way Kathy could use the connection.

30

I was getting nowhere, I needed to pause and take stock so I booked a court at the Montparnasse squash club. I went and hit a ball by myself, it helps me think.

What did we know about Zidane? Not much, but what we knew was not good.

He was planning a coup and he had a rich patron willing to finance him. You might think we could find the patron, get a line on the terrorist and stop him in his tracks.

Not happening, at least not yet.

While I was hitting, a stranger knocked on the glass door. "May I join you?"

You never know what to expect when someone does that. He could be good or bad, you can't tell. But good manners say you should agree and take whatever comes. It turned out he was a decent player but I was fitter than he was and we split four close games.

We had a drink in the bar. His name was Harry and he was something in real estate. He had a plan to open a squash club in the Tour Montparnasse.

He had probably been good looking once but he carried too much fat now, on both face and body. He struck me as lonely. He out-drank me by two to one and became expansive.

"Why are you here?" he asked, on his fourth gin and tonic.

"To play squash."

He frowned. "Why come all the way to Paris? Plenty of squash in London."

"I'd rather not say."

"Fair enough."

I moved my chair to get comfortable and it skidded a few inches on the damp tiles. As I leaned forward to keep my balance, my arm brushed Harry's glass which was near the edge of the table. It rolled off and fell towards the wet floor.

Then something happened so fast that I thought my eyes were playing tricks. Harry's hand shot out and caught the glass an inch from the ground. The weird thing was that he had been talking intently, looking me straight in the eye and not at the glass. He must have either 180 degree peripheral vision or amazing reflexes.

He replaced the glass and grinned. "Sorry," he said. "Another round?"

I shook my head. "I've had enough."

"Wise man." He patted his stomach. "I drink too much. Must get some of this weight off."

It struck me that his slowness around the squash court had nothing to do with his reactions which were lightning fast. The only handicap was his weight. If he lost thirty pounds he would beat me easily, but I had been able to steer the ball away from him. As a result he had usually been out of position. Yet he had still split our games.

"What did you say you did for a living?" I asked.

"Property development, lately."

"And before that?"

He hesitated. "Army."

"In what capacity?"

"Commandos."

"Did you see active service?"

"Some."

"Where?"

"Iraq, then Afghanistan."

"What happened? Did you quit?" I was being inquisitive to the point of rudeness but there was something about his manner, maybe just his reticence, that made me curious.

He nodded. "I reached the end of my contract. I could have re-upped but Afghanistan wasn't going to last much longer and the army was shrinking. I had to find a way of making a living so it was off to Civvy Street."

The old fashioned slang rang a faint bell. "Where did you go to school?" I asked.

He fidgeted. "A place called Bunnington. Then Cambridge."

I grinned. "I was at Bunnington."

He beamed. "Well fancy that. What's your last name?"

"Steele."

He looked at me closely. "I don't remember you."

"No reason why you should. You must be about 35?"

He nodded.

"That's five years older than me. You were probably a prefect when I was an ink-stained junior. What's *your* last name?"

"Hodge."

Things suddenly clicked. The solidly built man in front of me was *the* Hodge, a slim youth who was a gifted squash player and a fine boxer and rugby player as well. Hodge, not Harry. He had been a prefect and sports star my first year. First year nobodies like me didn't call gods by their Christian names.

He saw me staring and laughed. "Put on a few pounds, eh?"

"Sorry," I said. "I didn't make the connection."

"No problem. I know I'm not the pretty sixth-former of those days, but I just love to eat."

And drink, I thought. But I filed his name away in my mind. He could be useful. You never knew.

His gaze wandered over my shoulder and I turned to see a lissom black girl in turquoise tights walking off court, still sweating slightly.

He raised his voice. "Excuse me, miss."

She looked at him in surprise.

"I'm sorry to interrupt, but I just had to."

"Yes?"

"I've never done this before, but I must say that you are quite the most beautiful squash player I've ever set eyes on. Can we buy you a drink?"

I would have bet that she would refuse or at least ignore him. Wrong. She came and sat down.

Her name was Mireille and she was a postgraduate student from Burkina Faso studying mathematics at the Sorbonne.

"I won a maths scholarship to Cambridge," said Harry. He stumbled over *scholarship* but got the syllables out. "I spent a happy year there."

"That's not long," I said.

"I failed my exams."

"You won a scholarship and then got kicked out?"

"I was drunk."

He turned to Mireille. "I haven't slept with a woman in two weeks. Will you come back to my hotel?"

Would she slap his face? Apparently not. No reply, but he got a big smile for his pains.

He turned to me. "We could all go, what do you say?" His speech was clear but he swayed slightly.

I consulted my watch. "Can't make it, sorry. Got to go and shower."

When I came out of the locker room, the bar was

empty. Outside I was in time to see Mireille supporting Harry who was tottering into a cab. She followed him. I walked to the Metro station and went back to my hotel.

Kathy stirred cream into her latte and decided to call Rosie. She fired up her iPhone.

It emitted a repeating single tone, the kind that told her she was reaching the United States.

On the second ring she heard a familiar voice. "Hey baby, what's happening?"

"Hi Rosie, not much."

"Where are you?"

"In a Starbucks in Paris."

"Lucky you. I'm stewing here in L.A., up to my nose in textbooks and bored to death. What's up?"

"I'm on a project."

"What sort of project?"

"It involves counter-terrorism."

"How in Heaven's name did you get involved in something like that?"

"It's a long story. Listen, I need a favour. Which I'll make up to you."

"I'll do anything for a laugh, you know that."

"I want to use one of your connections."

"I didn't know I had any in Paris, but shoot!"

When it came to connections Rosie was something of a heavyweight. In most other ways she was quite the opposite, tall and slim with a model's figure. She favoured stiletto heels, choosing to accentuate her height, not hide it. Small breasted and straight backed, she piled her hair high on her head in a style reminiscent of her homeland.

She was very smart and much courted by the media who were intrigued by her combination of elegance and brains. She was currently studying for a PhD in political science and living by the beach in Santa Monica.

"You do have one Paris connection," said Kathy.

"Give me a clue."

"He isn't actually French."

"I'm drawing a blank."

"Like us, he studied in Los Angeles."

"Oh my god! Not Fredy?"

"Yep."

Kathy heard an audible sigh.

"Fredy Mifuba is rich, energetic and charming, but he's also a jerk."

"So I've heard."

"But you still want to meet him?"

"Yes, I do."

"May I ask why?"

Kathy was not sure how much to say.

"We think he's financing a very dangerous project. I could say more but it's probably better you don't know."

Rosie accepted this, being conditioned by years of experience in sub-Saharan politics. "Do you want to meet him in a social setting?"

"That would be best. Trouble is, you are in California and he is in Paris."

"Oh I don't want to be present, thanks very much."

"Will he meet me if you aren't there?"

"Are you kidding? A good looking white chick? He'll make a move on you of course. He's tried and failed with me so he wouldn't want me around, denting his tiny ego."

"Well, if you don't mind."

"No skin off my nose darling. Last time we met he drove me home in a Ferrari, bummed my last joint and propositioned me. I told him to bugger off which he didn't like. Hopefully, he'll have forgotten that. Anyway, I'll tell him to get in touch. Is this a good number?"

"Do you think he'll call?"

"Count on it. He's permanently as randy as hell."

"I don't know if you knew," said Kathy, "But the French Government just confiscated his dad's posh house on Avenue Victor Hugo as part of a corruption probe. Fredy's Rolls and his other cars were all impounded."

"All?"

"Except for one, a Ferrari. That's now his only transportation."

"The poor dear," said Rosie. "Ferraris are hell in traffic."

"How true," said Kathy. She was reminded that although Rosie had the common touch it was still a princess talking.

"He's moved in with a girlfriend," she said.

"Which one?"

"Katerina. The model."

"Oh, her."

"The point is, if I go to see him it'll be at her place."

"He'll probably suggest a spot of group hanky panky but I'm sure you can handle that."

As often with Rosie, Kathy was left wondering what she meant.

32

Rosie put down the phone.

She was sitting outside court two at the South Bay Squash Club in Torrance. She was a good player with excellent hand-eye coordination. She had just played five hard games with dermatologist Adrienne Brandriss, a former national champion.

After Adrienne left, Rosie stripped off her squash kit and, wrapping herself in a towel, went looking for the sauna.

She made a curious discovery: to get there she would have to walk through the men's locker room. But the club seemed deserted so she strolled through unobserved.

The sauna was warm from earlier use but the timer showed only a few minutes heat left so she twisted the dial to give herself another ten minutes, went in and perched on the teak bench. The dry wood was too hot for her bottom so she folded her towel in half and sat on it.

It took a few minutes for the heat to do its work. Then the pores opened and the sense of relaxation was sublime. But suddenly she heard men's voices. The door flew open.

Stuart Leslie and Mike Appleby, respectable married men, had been chatting in the street, enjoying the sunshine. They barged naked into the dimly lit sauna and collapsed on the bench before noticing the dusky presence in the corner.

"Hey fellas, what's happening?" Rosie asked cheerfully.

"Not much," muttered Appleby. History doesn't relate what passed through his mind but he chatted for five minutes with admirable sangfroid before leaving to get dressed.

Rosie re-wrapped herself before emerging, negotiated the men's locker room where both players smiled politely, and returned to the ladies side.

What an odd club, she thought to herself.

At home, she looked up Fredy in her leather address book and dialled his number.

33

Rosie's call must have done the trick because Kathy's phone rang an hour later with an invitation.

Next evening, dressed as smartly as the limits of her suitcase allowed, she found herself in the penthouse on Île Saint-Louis. Her game plan was simple: she didn't have one.

She looked around. It was pretty swish.

"Is this your place?" she asked.

Fredy shook his head. "You probably heard about the confiscation of our house on Victor Hugo. This is a friend's."

"He-friend or she-friend?"

He shrugged. "She."

Kathy said nothing. There was a pause. Finally, he said, "She's working today. She's a model."

"Ah."

She walked over to the window. In the darkness, floodlit Notre-Dame was reflected in the Seine.

"Want to offer me a drink?"

"Of course. Scotch?"

"Do you have any Campari?"

"Let me look." He disappeared into the kitchen.

His iPhone was sitting on the table. It was the identical model to her own. Acting completely on a whim, she scooped it up and replaced it with her own unit. Fredy's phone vanished into her purse.

She heard him opening and closing kitchen cabinets. A dreadful thought struck her. What if someone called him in the next few minutes? It would ring in her pocket. She fumbled for it and, cycling through the settings, set it on mute. She had barely finished and hidden it away when he returned.

"Campari." He brandished a bottle of the red liquor.

"Brilliant."

Armchairs and a sofa were arranged around a marble coffee table by the window. She deliberately avoided the sofa and perched on a chair. He sat on the sofa. She smiled.

She sensed his impatience. There was no doubt in her mind about what he would want next. Her game plan was to stay long enough not to seem rude while also managing to get the hell away, with his phone in her possession and her virtue intact. Keep talking!

But a short while later she looked at her watch. "It's late."

"You can stay here if you like," he said.

She smiled. "I'm most flattered but I'm in a committed relationship." Not true but what the heck.

He might as well not have heard her. "It's a cold night."

But she could not be persuaded. Muttering goodbyes, she was out of there at the speed of light.

On the street she looked round for a taxi. She was terrified that he would discover the deception with the phone. Finally, she sprinted for the Metro station, thanking her stars that he didn't know where she was staying.

She got off at Saint-Germain-des-Prés, went straight to Halfshaft's room at the Hôtel des Saints-Pères and hammered on his door. He answered, wearing sweat pants and a grubby T-shirt. The news was on television in French and he muted the sound.

She thrust Fredy's phone at him. "I need you to hack into this."

"No problem."

"You have to do it tonight."

"That's a problem."

"Why?"

"The WiFi signal here is weak, so I don't have the computing speed I need. I could go into the office but even then it would take several hours. What about tomorrow?"

"I guess that will have to do."

"What's the story?" he asked.

"That's Fredy Mifuba's phone. What I really need is a carbon copy of everything on it, so that I can return it in the morning and pretend I took it by mistake."

He laughed. "Why didn't you say so? I can duplicate it in a few minutes. Then I can work on the copy and give you the results later."

"How sure are you about that?"

"One hundred percent. Here, let me have that for a minute."

He reached for Mifuba's phone. Rummaging in his duffel bag, he produced a device the size of a paperback book, with a slot in one side. Connecting it to a power outlet, he slid the phone into the slot. The gadget hummed for thirty seconds and, when it fell quiet, a red diode winked on the console. He ejected the phone and handed it back to Kathy.

"Scary," she said. "Does that mean nobody's phone is secure?"

He shrugged. "Pretty much. When you buy a new phone, don't you get the people at the store to set it up for you?"

She nodded. "I guess so."

"What do they do? Don't they transfer your data across to the new machine, stuff like that?"

"Well, yes. But I assume they use confidential programs for that." She stared at him. "Well, don't they?"

He just grinned.

Next morning she almost telephoned Mifuba. Then she remembered that the number she had for him was for the device she had stolen, which was sitting on her nightstand.

So she e-mailed him instead, full of apologies, saying she would return it by messenger within the hour.

He replied saying tersely, "Okay!"

She duly sent it back with one of Goldhawk's employees. She didn't know if Mifuba would suspect that he had been duped. She was afraid he might, but even if he did it was too late to do anything about it.

34

I took a taxi to Boulevard de Montmorency next morning.

Madame peered out of her lair in the lodge, frowning. "Yes?"

"I am a friend of the young woman who came and spoke to you yesterday."

"What do you want?"

"That man who was here, Dutrieux. I wish to speak to him."

"It's a free country."

"Which apartment is he in?"

She shrugged. "I don't recall."

The French can be pretty bloody when they want to. I took out my wallet. Her eyes followed it.

"Do you have a favourite charity, Madame?"

She said nothing. I took out a twenty euro note. Still no reaction.

I took out another twenty, then put the wallet back in my pocket with a flourish designed to show finality.

"Little Sisters of the Poor," she said.

"Excellent choice." I handed over a note, which vanished into her purse. I kept the other in full view.

"Un instant." She picked up the phone.

"M. Dutrieux? Il y a quelqu'un ici qui voudrait vous parler."

A pause.

"He says he's a friend of the American woman who was looking for M. Chaudry yesterday."

She replaced the receiver. "He's coming down."

I waited until I heard footsteps on the stairs before handing her the second banknote. She still hung around.

"This is a private conversation," I said.

She marched back into her room and slammed the door.

Mr. Dutrieux shook hands. He seemed sociable and good natured. A pleasant change. I'd had enough fraught meetings recently.

"I'd like to talk to Munir Chaudry," I said. "I think you told my colleague that he played squash."

"That's right."

"How good is he?"

"Not bad. Do you play?"

"I played number three for Oxford six years ago."

"I'm impressed."

"I'm a bit rusty now."

"Actually, Chaudry should be back in town today. He has to play his semi-final in the club championship."

"Which club?"

"The CMG Sports Club on Rue de Rennes in Montparnasse."

"I wouldn't mind watching some good squash."

Dutrieux laughed. "I don't know how good it will be by your standards, but come along if you want."

"Are spectators allowed?"

"No problem, come as my guest."

I was in the gallery watching as Munir Chaudry played his match. He looked pumped and energetic. His opponent was one Greg Stiles, an American visitor.

It was a close-fought affair. Stiles was the older player. He wore hinged braces on both knees which did not bode well for his chances. He looked slow at first, losing the first two games in the best-of-five format. But he drew level at two games apiece, thanks to a series of straight drives to the back of the court and the occasional pinpoint drop shot.

In the fifth and final game, greater experience enabled him to draw ahead of an increasingly tired Chaudry. He finished things off with a spectacular three-wall nick that had the gallery gasping. He acknowledged the applause graciously. The match lasted three quarters of an hour and by the end, both players were exhausted.

Afterwards, I went into the locker room where Chaudry sat bathed in sweat. I stood in front of him.

"I watched your match. Well played!"

He looked up. "Thank you. Have we met?"

"No, but we have a mutual friend."

"Who is that?"

It was crunch time.

"Omar Chadeau."

If you've ever seen a balloon deflate slowly after being punctured, the surface shrivelling, that was Chaudry's face.

I was almost sorry for him, but not quite. "We should talk."

He looked around wild-eyed, not sure whether I was friend or foe. I could have been a friend of Zidane-Chadeau, bringing a message from the man. Or I could have been the authorities, come to arrest him.

In fact, I was neither but he clearly realised that to be called out in the changing room at his squash club was a shocking breach of security.

"Not here," I said. "There's a bistro around the corner, Chez Panisse. Get showered but don't take long. I'll be waiting."

He nodded mutely. When he saw that I was preparing to leave, I spotted a glimmer of hope in his eye. I turned back quickly. "Don't change your mind," I said. "It wouldn't be prudent." I got a scowl in return.

· · ·

Chez Panisse happens to be a favourite of mine. No point in slumming it. I asked the waiter for a table in a quiet corner and ordered a plate of Escargots à la Bourguignonne.

I was sipping a Kir when Chaudry arrived. He came and sat down.

"Something to drink?" I asked.

He glared at me. "There had better be a good explanation for this."

He had summoned some bravado but there were worry lines at the corners of his eyes. He looked about forty although he had acted younger on the squash court.

"You are the one who needs to explain," I said.

"Explain what?"

"Why the diplomat of a nuclear power is talking to a known terrorist in a city like Paris that has a large Muslim population?"

"I am doing nothing of the kind."

"We have telephone records."

"That is impossible."

"They are not from your phone."

"Whose, then?"

I smiled and shook my head.

His drink arrived, Scotch. A secular Muslim.

"Who are you, anyway?" he gritted.

I produced a card, which he studied.

"Financial Investigations! Should I be intimidated?"

It was not really a question, more of a sneer. I've been thinking I should get some new cards, actually. Mine are on the flippant side, a good ice-breaker and okay for everyday use but this time they could lead us in the wrong direction.

"So, Mr. Investigator, who is your client?"

"That doesn't matter. What does matter is that a word to the authorities would land you in serious trouble."

For the first time since we met, a tentative look of relief spread over his face.

"Is it money you want?"

I said nothing.

He misunderstood my silence. "How much?"

"Sorry," I said, "It's not that simple. But speaking of money, how much did Chadeau, who by the way is actually a terrorist called Zidane, pay you?"

It was a shot in the dark but it hit home. He flushed.

"That was never the point. It is the principal. A gesture must be made."

He sounded sincere, but clearly there was some kind of conflict going on. I was pretty sure that, whatever he might say, money had played a part.

At this point, the discussion grew curiously less hostile. The atmosphere was still tense but the bluster and threats were gone.

"Look," I said, "You decided for whatever reason to take a wrong step. But I can't let you go through with it. You have to tell me what's going on. It's not negotiable."

He stared into space. Finally, he dropped his head on his chest and a sob escaped.

I looked around. The waiter was staring. I was afraid

that if he burst into loud tears, we might be asked to leave and I had escargots coming. "Pull yourself together!" I said.

He sniffed and blew his nose on his napkin. "I needed the money."

"How much?"

He looked evasive. "He paid the funds to me. I negotiated a price with the engineers. The difference was mine to keep."

"What engineers?"

"The people in Pakistan."

The waiter brought my snails but, I have to say, I almost didn't enjoy them. For the first time I felt real dread. Chaudry had just told me that he had set in train a nuclear disaster because he was short of money. It blew the mind. It was not really important how much he had stolen for himself. The priority was to prevent the horror threatening the city.

I leaned forward. "Let's be clear. You have conspired to commit terrorism. There will be penalties. But at least you can make some amends."

"How?"

"By helping us stop this thing. Where is Zidane? What is he doing? How much time do we have?"

He stared as if shell-shocked.

"Come on, where is he?"

"I don't know."

"Where does he live?"

"I was never told."

"You are lying. Where did your meetings take place?"

"In public places, cafes. He would telephone and tell me where and when. Then he would appear. When we were done, he would leave. I never knew where he went."

"What kind of device are we talking about?"

"It is essentially a suitcase-sized bomb, suitable to be smuggled into France and detonated in a public place."

"What public place?"

"I was not told."

"But here in Paris?"

He nodded.

"When?"

"As soon as possible, I guess."

I was thinking furiously. "You said the explosion will be here. But you live here. How will you know when to leave the city?"

He said nothing.

"Or do you plan to be a martyr to the cause and let yourself be incinerated along with everyone else?" My sarcasm was deliberate.

He shook his head. "He will call and warn me when things are imminent."

Good luck with that, I thought. Putting myself in Zidane's shoes for a moment, I knew exactly how much warning I would give the wretched Chaudry – none. He would be collateral damage, a loose end conveniently tidied up by the explosion.

"Who is your contact in Pakistan?" I asked.

"A nuclear engineer in the Ministry of Defence."

"I need a name."

He scowled, but self-doubt was destroying his resistance. "Mirza. His name is Rashid Mirza."

"How do you know him?"

"We were at university together in London."

"What is his motivation in all this?"

"Like me, he is a believer."

"And like you, willing to profit from his belief?"

He shrugged. "I suppose so."

"Does he know where the device is going to be used?"

Chaudry shook his head. "I let him believe that it would be used in Somalia."

"Somalia?"

"Why not? Somalia is a failed state, a country in chaos. The regime, such as it is, is not one that would inspire sympathy among Pakistani engineers."

"I shall need your contact's address." I pulled a piece of paper and a pencil from my pocket, and pushed them towards him.

His glass was empty and I ordered more whiskey. I was pushing my luck as far as it would go. He was clearly very volatile emotionally and at the moment he was being cooperative, thanks to my threats and his own belated grasp of the enormity of what he had done. He was no professional terrorist. If he was, he would have been a tougher nut to crack and unlikely to be intimidated by an amateur like me.

But meanwhile, any information I could extract, by bluff or by alcohol, I would willingly accept.

Slowly he wrote a name, address and phone number and handed it back. I looked at it.

"This is in English."

"Yes."

"Write it in Urdu."

"Why? Educated Pakistanis all speak English."

"What about taxi drivers?"

He gave me a look of grudging respect and added a few lines of demotic script.

I pocketed it and stood up.

"What are you going to do?"

I smiled. "None of your business." But I actually had no idea.

"What should I do?"

"I'll let you know."

I left him staring at a full tumbler of whiskey which I guessed would not last long.

35

After listening at supper to what Steele and Kathy were doing, Kon Feaver had some thoughts of his own. He went to the hotel concierge and asked for directions to the nearest reference library.

What was M'sieu looking for exactly?

"I need biographical material on the model Katerina Arnau. I am a journalist doing a background piece for this year's shows."

The concierge wrote the address on a pad and tore off the page.

"Here, it's only ten minutes' walk. But if I may suggest . . ."

"Yes?"

The concierge reached behind his desk and produced a folded newspaper which he handed to Kon. "This you can read immediately. It's just a scandal sheet but it's got some good stuff."

Kon scanned the tabloid. It was in French but there were a lot of pictures and the words were not complicated so he got the gist. Katerina was a leading model who could earn twenty thousand dollars a day just for smiling in front of a camera. It mentioned her major accounts which ranged from perfume to cars, cosmetics and her own line of lingerie, Katerina Intimates.

"I'd like to interview her," he said.

The concierge nodded. "So would I. Good luck with that!" He laughed.

Kon telephoned Tisch. "Didn't you say Goldhawk had investments in publishing?"

"Sure. He owns thirty percent of International Magazines."

"Do they cover fashion?"

"Some of them do, I guess."

"Perfect."

Within a couple of hours, Kon was the proud owner of a press pass as Associate Fashion Editor of 'Belle,' a popular lowbrow fashion rag. Thus armed, he telephoned the office of Katerina's agent, Rudi Sachs.

"She's too busy to do press today," said Rudi curtly.

"Tomorrow would be fine."

"Or tomorrow."

Kon sighed apologetically. "We heard that she's living with Fredy Mifuba who just had his house confiscated for money-laundering. Just wanted to be sure she wasn't implicated. Hate her to get unfair negative press."

"She had nothing to do with any of that," snapped Rudi.

'But the rumour is out there. A chance for her to deny it face to face would sure be good for her image."

Kon let the thought hang. The implication that the reverse would also be true was not lost on Rudi.

After a long pause, he said, "I can let you have ten minutes with her tomorrow morning."

"That's not much."

"It's the best I can do. You'll have to go to her place of work, she's shooting a Harley Davidson commercial. You can try and catch her during a break."

Next morning, he was in a hangar filled with flood-lights, Harley Davidson bikes and all the paraphernalia of a full-scale fashion shoot. Katerina had been warned of his presence. He had prepared some conventional fashion-type questions which she answered politely but without much enthusiasm.

Finally, he put his pencil and notepad away.

"Thanks," he said. Then, "Oh, one more thing. Did you know that Fredy Mifuba has been talking to a known terrorist?"

Katerina froze. Several things fell into place.

"That's absurd," she said, but the words did not carry conviction.

"I'm afraid it's true," said Kon.

"Who are you, anyway?" she snapped.

"I'm just a reporter. But that doesn't matter. Let me ask, have you seen him talking to anyone new lately?"

Things clicked in her mind. The uninvited visit from Zidane. Her discomfort with him. The snatches of phone conversation with Fredy. It was all a big jumble in her head and she couldn't make sense of it all but something told her it wasn't good.

She looked Kon in the eye for the first time. To her surprise, she liked what she saw. His face had a quizzical, lived-in look, with a skin like leather, a thick dark head of hair greying at the temples. Laugh lines at the corners of his eyes made her feel like trusting him. On the other hand . . .

"I can't tell you anything, you're a complete stranger."

"A stranger who could help you."

A director's assistant poked his head around the door. "You're on, Katerina."

She stood up.

Kon wrote his name and phone number on the back page of a magazine. He tore off the strip and handed it to her. "This will find me if you want to talk."

It wasn't much but at least he had got her attention. He went and had lunch.

36

October 16th

Katerina was in her bedroom a few days later when she heard Fredy's phone ring and the sound of him talking.

He came in and said, "It's Zidane, he's coming round."

"Why?"

She heard the anxiety in her own voice. The idea of facing Zidane scared her.

"I don't know. I guess he has some details to talk over."

"I don't care for him," she said.

He looked sharply at her. "He's all right."

"He makes me uncomfortable," she said. "And this *is* my place."

"He won't stay long."

She felt foolish but also resentful. Fredy was treating her with disrespect and it was happening more and more lately. He went to the counter and poured himself coffee from a flask she had just brewed.

"Aren't you going to work today?" he asked. As if he wanted her gone, as if she was unwelcome in her own flat.

She shook her head. "My next shoot is the day after tomorrow."

It was all too much. She went into the bathroom, locked the door, and telephoned Kon Feaver.

37

K on heard nothing from Katerina for several days. He worried that he should not have left things so open with her but finally the phone rang early in the morning.

He had just brewed coffee, using the machine in his hotel room.

"Is this Kon Feaver?" She sounded breathless and scared.

"Sure is."

"This is Katerina. We met the other day."

"How could I forget?"

"Listen, I'd like to talk."

"I'm all ears."

"You said something about bad things happening."

"I did."

"You obviously know more than you were saying. I

don't know who you work for, whether it's the police or what, but . . . "

"It's 'or what.'"

"Huh?"

An Israeli should not have tried to make a verbal joke in English with a Brazilian in Paris but Kon didn't have much self-restraint about that kind of thing. "I'm sorry. Speak!"

"A man came to my apartment last week to see Fredy."

"A man?"

"He and Fredy are planning something and it's not good."

"What makes you say that?"

"I've heard them on the phone. Fredy is furious at the French authorities and he's the sort of person who might do something really stupid."

"And the other man is helping him?"

"I think so."

"In what way?"

I don't know, I just have a feeling. The guy was waiting in my flat a few days ago even though he doesn't have a key, sitting in my living room as if he owned the place. It gave me the creeps. Now he wants to come round again."

"Would you like me to be there?"

"Could you? I live on Île Saint-Louis."

Kon felt an adrenaline rush. "Well, it would even out the numbers. If this man and Fredy are up to something uncool, maybe you and I together can put a spoke in their wheel."

"He is on his way here now."

"I'm on it," said Kon. "What's the guy's name, by the way?"

"Zidane."

"Give me twenty minutes."

After their first meeting in the Meurice bar, Tisch had taken Kon back to his suite and handed him a Beretta 9mm pistol. "You might need this, you never know," he said. Now, before leaving, Kon went and retrieved it. He had stowed it in the small combination safe in the bottom of the clothes closet in his bedroom along with several clips of ammunition. He loaded it with a fifteen shot clip, put the safety catch on and slipped it into the pocket of his leather jacket where it hardly made a bulge.

He also made a brief phone call, leaving a message on the recipient's voicemail. Then, satisfied, he left the room and headed for Île Saint-Louis.

Katerina checked her appearance in the bathroom mirror. She made a conscious effort to look unconcerned. She felt ridiculous. Was she panicking for no reason? She unlocked the door and strolled casually back into the living room.

Fredy had gone out on the balcony to smoke a cigarette. He was leaning on the rail and gazing down at the silver river, touched by the morning sun. His ebony face was expressionless.

He was still there when Zidane arrived a few minutes later. Katerina let him in. The Algerian smiled his wordless smile as he entered.

"He's on the balcony," she said shortly. "You can go out. Would you like coffee?"

He shook his head and went over to the full length sliding door and out onto the balcony. He closed the door behind him, cutting off the sound between the balcony and the rest of the flat.

She could see the men talking, but not hear them. Their expressions gave no clue as to what they were saying but the tableau suggested disagreement of some kind. Once or twice Zidane gestured indoors as if referring to Katerina and Fredy shook his head.

The buzzer rang downstairs. She pressed the intercom.

"Here I am," said Kon. "Lovely morning."

She buzzed him in and opened the apartment door a crack so that he could walk in when he got upstairs. Feeling more confident, she moved towards the balcony and, sliding open the glass door, stepped outside.

Mifuba and Zidane turned in surprise.

"Look, I think I deserve to know what is going on," she blurted.

The men exchanged glances.

"I told you, it's a business matter," said Mifuba.

"Just business?"

"That's right."

"Then why the secrecy? I don't mind dressing up and going through that pantomime in the brasserie but I want to know why. What's going on? I don't appreciate being a pawn in someone else's chess game."

"There's no secret, it's just normal discretion." But Mifuba sounded weak and defensive.

Zidane said, "Fredy and I are working on a project in the import-export field."

"Really? A source tells me there may be some element of violence."

She regretted the words instantly but they had slipped out. She was over-wrought, not in control.

The silence that followed was of a whole new quality. She realized with dismay that one unfortunate word had fundamentally changed her relationship with Mifuba which until then, while not warm, had been more or less sociable.

"What source is that?" asked Zidane.

"It's not important. I talk to a lot of people."

"That's absurd," said Mifuba. His eyes flickered to Zidane.

He smiled but there was enough uncertainty about his expression to reinforce Katerina's worst fears. She sensed that, although Mifuba had more physical presence, besides being wealthier, the older man was the real leader.

Zidane shook his head sorrowfully. "I am sorry you should think that." Again the smile, almost apologetic.

He raised a hand and took a step towards Katerina. She backed away.

The lift rose, smooth and silent. Like everything about the building it felt solid and well maintained. Kon took out the gun and undid the safety catch before replacing it loosely in his jacket. Then, hands in pockets, he strolled nonchalantly into the flat.

He took in what was happening on the balcony. Katerina was wrestling with a slightly built man in a raincoat. Another man, African, stood nearby, watching but making no attempt to interfere.

Katerina was tall and slender. Her job required her to follow a strict diet so there was no spare weight on her and Zidane clearly had the physical advantage. He seemed to be pushing her before him. She had wrapped her arms around him, but she seemed to have no real idea of how to defend herself.

Kon sprinted across the living room and burst onto the balcony.

The two men were preoccupied and did not see him until he was a few feet away. By then, for Katerina, the die was cast.

Zidane had prised her arms from around his waist. Crouching down, he gathered and lifted her jean-clad thighs and got her up and over the bronze railing of the balcony. Grunting, he gave her a hard shove.

Katerina sailed slowly up and backwards. Her frantic gaze fixed on Kon, recognition mixed with terrified understanding of what was happening. Still yards away, Kon flung out a hand as she fell silently from view.

He rushed to the edge of the balcony in the faint hope that her fall might have been arrested on a lower floor, but the trajectory had been outwards and, as he looked down, he could see the slim body lying spread-eagled on the pavement six floors below.

His first thought was to dash downstairs in case something could be done to help but he was immediately aware of the gun held by Zidane, which was trained at his chest.

"Let me go down."

Zidane shook his head. "There's nothing to be done, I'm afraid. Such a shame . . ."

"You bastard," Kon muttered, but he was checked by the gun.

Zidane shrugged. "As they say in novels, you have the advantage of me. I don't know you, although I think you know who I am."

"You are Zidane."

The little man nodded. "Which is why, as you must understand, I have to dispose of you."

'As you disposed of her?" said Kon.

"I'm afraid so."

Kon motioned towards Mifuba who had been looking on impassively. "What about him?"

Zidane was silent.

Mifuba smiled. "We are joined at the hip."

What a pair, thought Kon.

He had been in tight spots before, and taken risks. They had not always worked, which was one reason he had not been a huge success in the military, but nobody had ever questioned his nerve. He had to take a risk now.

He staggered, and fell slightly towards Zidane, eyes closing, tongue hanging out. As he collapsed on the hard floor of the balcony, he appeared to be fainting or having a seizure. Zidane recoiled and his gun arm wavered. That was enough for Kon. His arms flailed, seemingly uncoordinated, but his fist batted the gun away. It slid along the balcony. Kon straightened up and faced Zidane.

"Now then."

But he had forgotten Mifuba who sprang to life and scooped up the gun. From the corner of his eye, he sensed rather than saw Mifuba. The Kongolan swung the gun barrel at the back of Kon's head.

It connected with a sickening thud and the Israeli collapsed, this time for real.

39

I picked up Kon's message just after breakfast. It was a fine morning and I had gone down to the hotel courtyard for coffee and a croissant in the sunshine. It was not until I got back to the room that I checked my voicemail.

"Just heard from Katerina Arnau. Going round to her place. Might need moral support."

It was timed half an hour ago. Kon did not sound too stressed, but then he never did.

The streets were crowded with rush hour traffic, so I took the Metro. It was half an hour before I reached her building and went up in the lift. The apartment door was ajar so I went in.

For the second time in a week, I bumped into Mifuba. He was carrying a suitcase and brushed past me, heading towards the lift.

Kon had been tied to a radiator with some kind of thin cord. An older man in a raincoat was holding a gun, apparently about to shoot him. I didn't know what Zidane looked like but it had to be him. There was no sign of Katerina.

Zidane whipped around. He aimed the gun at me and fired. The shot smacked into some expensive panelling behind my head and I took cover behind a bookcase.

I never served in the military but I've come under fire several times and, frankly, I find the experience terrifying. The Cato brothers from Colombia tried to kill me twice, once on Antigua by machine-gunning my car, and again on Guadeloupe when Kon and I hunted them on the slopes of the Soufrière volcano.

Each time, my survival was due not so much to courage but to that electric boost in reaction time that comes from a desperate urge to survive. Terror sure can save one's skin. If you want to call that bravery, feel free. Anyway, it did the trick.

I couldn't see Zidane but I crouched down to present the smallest possible target while I attended to Kon. I grabbed a kitchen knife and cut him loose. It was plastic clothes line and the knife went through it like butter. I heard the door creak and saw Zidane hurrying out after Mifuba.

Kon muttered, "Follow them. Shoot the bastards."

I left him rubbing the circulation back into his wrists and dashed out into the corridor but I was too late to catch the lift, which I could hear descending.

I ran back to the flat and out onto the balcony, where Kon joined me.

We looked down. The yellow Ferrari was drawing away in a burst of noise. A woman's body lay spread-eagled on the pavement and a crowd was starting to gather.

"What the Sam Hill is going on?" I said.

"Where do I begin?"

"Is that Katerina's body?"

He nodded. "Poor kid. Her only crime was knowing where Zidane lives. For that she had to die. Now, nobody knows – except Mifuba, I guess."

"Fill me in."

He nodded. "I had an interesting chat with Mr. Zidane. A bit one sided because I had just been hit on the head and had my hands tied together. Thanks for turning up, by the way."

"No problem."

"Anyway, your guess about a nuclear device was right on the mark. The plan is to import a powerful bomb and set it off somewhere in Paris."

"With Mifuba providing the money?"

"Of course. Zidane is taking advantage of Mifuba's pathological hatred of the French."

"How much money?"

Kon shrugged. "A lot."

"That's bad. Presumably the bigger the cost, the bigger the bomb," I said.

He nodded.

I held up a hand. "Before we go any further, a question. What do we do now, as in the next ten minutes?"

"By rights, we should make a full report to the police."

"By rights."

Our eyes met. Kon said, "The thing is, you were not a witness. I was, but I don't know how I can help the police.

"Katerina is gone and we can't bring her back to life."

"If we stay here we'll get tangled up with the police," I said.

"Might even be treated as suspects."

"Is there a back entrance to this place?" I asked.

"We could have a look."

We did, and there was.

The news next day:

"Top model plunges to death."

"Accident, or something else?"

"Ferrari seen leaving death scene on Île Saint-Louis."

"Police are anxious to interview Francois Mifuba, also known as Fredy, son of the president of Kongolo whose luxury home was recently impounded by fiscal authorities."

Tisch cross-examined us.

"You say this pair of maniacs got clean away?"

"That's about it."

"So we're back to square one."

"As far as finding them, yes."

"A yellow Ferrari is pretty conspicuous," said Tisch.

I nodded. "My guess is that the first thing they will do is separate, they are both lone wolves. Then, Mifuba will hide the Ferrari. He just needs a house with a garage. He'll take the Ferrari there under cover of darkness and leave it."

"He'll probably skip the country," said Kon. "He's not popular in Paris to put it mildly, so why hang around?"

Kathy was listening. "Won't they be watching out for him at airports?"

"He may have a private plane," I said.

Tisch said, "Mifuba is not the most important thread in this tangled ball. He's only there to pay for stuff. Zidane is the main actor."

"And we don't know where he is," said Kathy.

"And the clock is ticking," said Mimi.

There was a glum silence.

Tisch looked at his watch. He was sending a message, which was, *it's getting late and Mimi and I wouldn't mind some privacy*. Kathy and I got up to leave.

We went out onto Rue de Rivoli for some fresh air.

Our eyes met.

"Your hotel or mine?" I asked hopefully.

She looked thoughtful. "I guess I wouldn't mind seeing how you *Rive Gauche* folks live."

"Okay," I said. Keep cool now.

"What I really want is some dinner," she said.

I chose *Aux Prés* **in the Rue du Dragon,** mainly because it was just a few minutes' walk from my hotel. It was also the right size for a restaurant in my view – small and intimate. The bell captain at the hotel said the veal was amazing and he turned out to be right.

Kathy was still in jeans but was sporting yet another T-shirt, this time pledging allegiance to the Boston Celtics. She scanned the room with a sort of high energy watchfulness, then nodded at me. She was keeping her guard up in more ways than one, I thought.

We ate slowly, chatting about this and that and then I paid the bill. We stood up, Kathy linking her arm in mine as if we were old friends.

We took a stroll by the Seine. In the Celtics shirt, Kathy pushed closer to me for warmth. It made us clumsy.

I said, "Are you supporting me?"

She said, "I want to."

We strolled back to the hotel, relaxed, not rushing. We waited for the elevator and went up to the room. Then things got less relaxed and more personal. In bed Kathy was warm and energetic and American – eventually she fell asleep. I decided that I liked her a lot and she seemed to like me, and then I fell asleep too.

"Oliver," she said later.

"Yes?"

"I was just trying it out, it's a good name."

"What should I call you?" I asked.

"Kathy's fine. Or, 'hey you,' I'm not particular."

40

Zidane and Fredy stood on the sidewalk outside Katerina's apartment.

"Get into the car," snapped Fredy.

Zidane clambered in awkwardly, he was not used to riding in a Ferrari. They drove off at high speed.

Both men were aware that things had got out of hand. Their project was at risk and they must proceed carefully.

"Who the hell were those two guys?" asked Fredy.

"As to the second, I have no idea," said Zidane. "The first one was an Israeli. His name is Feaver and he comes from Florida."

"How do you know?"

"I took these from him." Zidane produced a wallet and opened it to show a driver's license and credit cards.

"Let me see." Fredy grabbed the wallet and stared at the driver's license in a folding transparent panel inside. It showed a smiling Kon, full face, and announced his address as Coquina Key, Florida.

Fredy's concentration was diverted from the road and he nearly drove up onto the sidewalk, but corrected the Ferrari with a violent swerve. In the confusion, the wallet flew out of his hand and fell on the floor underneath his seat. He felt for it but could not reach it in the cramped cabin, and neither could Zidane.

"Don't worry, we'll get it later," snapped Fredy. He was driving fast.

"Slow down," said Zidane.

"We need to get away from that place," Fredy growled.

"I understand that. What we don't need is to get booked for speeding. We have very little time before some well-meaning bystander calls the police."

Fredy thought of Katerina's body lying in a crumpled heap on the sidewalk. He felt a twinge of sorrow, she had been kind, taken him in. They had some good times. If only she had kept her nose out of his business. The twinge passed.

"Shall I take you to your place?" he offered.

Zidane shook his head. "Just set me down."

He was thinking, *this guy is hard to control, I need to put some distance between us.* But Fredy was part of the plan and would remain so until Zidane was sure he no longer needed him. He had already separated the surly Kongolan from two million dollars but there might be a need for more, you never knew.

"You must do something about this car, it's too conspic-uous," he said.

Fredy saw the sense in that. But he didn't like being patronised by the older man. "I know what I'm doing," he said. The car screeched to a halt.

Zidane got out. "We'll talk," he said, leaning over the low slung vehicle.

Fredy nodded at him out of the window.

Zidane waved, turned, and walked away.

In the excitement, he had left Kon Feaver's wallet lying under Fredy's seat on the floor of the Ferrari. He remem-bered it a minute later but by then the Ferrari was out of sight. He shrugged his shoulders, resigned. It probably didn't matter.

Fredy drove until he saw a multi-story carpark. He entered it, taking a ticket from an automated gate. There was a glass attendant's kiosk, but it was empty. That was good. He drove up several floors of the concrete structure looking for a suitable space. He chose one in a corner, poorly lit and inconspicuous, drove into it and switched off the engine.

He took out his phone – there were calls he must make. But first, he got out and rummaged in the trunk of the Ferrari. He found what he wanted, a car cover made of heavy leather-finish plastic, suitable for putting over the car to protect it from dust. He seldom used it – he had servants who washed and polished the vehicle daily – but now it would be perfect. He gathered his suitcase and belongings, remembering to retrieve Kon Feaver's wallet, then draped the cover over the Ferrari, hiding its bright yellow bodywork in a dark cloak of anonymity.

He took the elevator down to the ground floor. As he was leaving he passed the table of prices. Rates were quoted by the hour and by the day. There was no mention of a maximum time limit, but clearly, stays of several days were envisioned. He could probably count on the car not being noticed for some time and in fact he never intended to use it again. A pity, he had only owned the car for a few months and was quite fond of it.

He stood on the sidewalk and phoned his attorney.

Fabrice Hannay, attorney and counsellor to the Republic of Kongolo, and to the Mifuba family in particular, was about to leave his office for a long lunch but when his secretary told him who it was he took the call immediately.

Hannay was shifty by nature and it showed in his appearance. Plump faced and with a slightly hunted look, he was fifty pounds overweight, although his well cut suit did a good job of making that less obvious. He had a quick and obsequious smile which he could deploy in an instant for a favoured client but he could also turn it off in a flash, replacing it with a scowl when grilling some ill-prepared adversary in court, peppering him with non sequiturs of little legal weight but effective in confusing his adversary.

The Mifubas were by far his most profitable account –

between legal advice, political lobbying and some even shadier stuff, their business was worth several million dollars a year.

"Fredy dear boy, how nice to hear from you, what's up?"

"I'm coming round. I need your help."

"Of course. You can rely on me, you know that." Lunch would have to wait.

"For starters, I need a car and a place to live."

Hannay blinked but recovered quickly. "Bring your driver's license. I'll have my secretary call some agents for details of houses to look at."

"You don't understand," said Fredy. "I don't want to give my license details."

"But in France, to rent a car, it is necessary to provide that information."

Fredy's voice rose. "I told you no! Rent the car in another name, your own perhaps. It must not be traceable to me."

Hannay shifted gear into ultra-servile. "Of course. I promised your father I would look after you and I will, dear friend. Don't worry about a thing. I'll see you shortly."

He turned to his secretary. "Two things. First, he wants to rent a house. Get some particulars. It should be the very best and in a good neighbourhood, say Neuilly or Le Vésinet."

She nodded. "Furnished?"

"A good point. Yes. And for immediate use."

"That will narrow the field."

"Can't be helped. Do the best you can."

"What is the second thing?"

"A car. And that must be in your name."

She hesitated. "Let me get this straight. I rent the car in my name, but he will drive it?"

"Don't worry. If there's a problem I will indemnify you."

"I don't like the idea."

"You don't have to. Now get on with it."

Arrangements were made and that afternoon Fredy called at Hannay's office in Place de la Madeleine.

He nodded as Hannay handed him the keys to a shiny Lexus saloon.

"It's rented in Giselle's name." He indicated his secretary who smiled uncertainly. "If you are stopped for any reason, she's a friend who lent it to you and forgot to tell Hertz. Better still, drive carefully and don't get stopped, then you won't have to lie."

Fredy nodded. "What about the house?"

Hannay showed him three one-page summaries. "Here are some to check out, let me know when you would like to go and see them."

Fredy shook his head. "No time for that." He looked briefly at each, then tapped one with his finger.

Photos showed a gravel driveway leading to a well kept brick and stone house.

"This will do."

Hannay turned an expression of surprise into congratulation. "Wise choice, I liked that one too."

"Next thing." Fredy produced Kon Feaver's wallet. "I want you to find this person."

Hannay read the Florida address on the driver's license and sucked his teeth. "Do you know where he is?"

"If I knew, I wouldn't be asking you."

"Is he in Paris?"

"Probably, but I have no idea where."

Hannay emptied the wallet's contents onto the desk – fifty euros in folding money, a couple of credit cards with the same Florida address, the card from a Paris restaurant and a creased scrap of till roll which he straightened out and studied, squinting through his bifocals.

"He appears to be staying at the Meurice, or at least eating there."

"Find out more about him. Why is he in France? Who does he associate with?"

Hannay spread his hands in frustration. "How would I know such things?"

"That's up to you. It's what I pay you for."

Hannay stifled a frown. "Very well."

"One more thing," said Fredy.

"Yes?"

"I need some firearms. For self-defence, you understand."

"Of course," Fabrice Hannay's eyes flickered in his fleshy face and he glanced at his secretary and lowered his voice. He put an arm round Fredy's shoulders and ushered him outside. They stood in the panelled hallway talking quietly for a few minutes.

· · ·

Fredy drove the Lexus away from Hannay's office. It was a smart vehicle, although much less eye-catching than the yellow Ferrari. He parked it in the driveway of his new house in Neuilly-sur-Seine where it suited the surroundings well – his cover was excellent, he thought. He had merged imperceptibly into the world of the well-to-do upper middle classes.

The place belonged to a South American diplomat home on leave and in need of cash. It had been hurriedly cleaned, heated and equipped with food and drink. He helped himself to a large scotch and settled down to wait. He was expecting a call from Hannay.

His phone rang. It was the attorney.

"What's the story?" asked Fredy.

"I sent an agent to the hotel. He spotted Feaver in the lobby, talking to an older man. My agent spoke to the check-in desk and it turns out the other man is Carlton Tisch, an American who is staying there with his wife."

"And who is this Tisch?"

"I thought you would ask. He's clearly someone of means – the Meurice is expensive – so we ran his name through a business database. It turns out he is the president of a large company called Eastern Debt Factors."

"Never heard of it."

"You might have if you were a manufacturing business in the United States. It is one of the biggest commercial lenders with a market value of twenty billion dollars."

Fredy was silent. It was obvious, to him at least, that Tisch was calling the shots. Kon Feaver was probably just an agent of the wealthier man. Fredy had a healthy respect for anyone whose riches matched or exceeded his own. It was the mindset of a bully and like any bully he immediately tried to think of ways to overcome his adversary, by foul means if necessary.

At first, nothing came to mind. But one thing was clear. Zidane was his best chance for revenge on the nation that had humiliated him and if Tisch threatened that plan, Tisch must go. Kill the beast and the rest of the opposition would crumble.

"I shall need your man to point out Tisch for me. I'll take matters from there."

"No problem," said Hannay. He was no fool and he knew of the Mifuba family's penchant for violence. But he had no scruples himself and as long as he was not personally at risk, whatever Fredy might do was a matter of indifference to him.

It was agreed that Fredy would meet Hannay's agent at the Meurice next day.

They stood together in the lobby of the Meurice next morning, the Kongolan and the nondescript Frenchman who was Hannay's agent. The agent had been able to snap some candid camera photos with his iPhone, which he showed Fredy and when, after half an hour, Tisch emerged from an elevator with a young woman who Fredy assumed was his wife, they were able to follow him without being seen.

Tisch and Mimi had decided – or rather Mimi had decided – that Tisch needed an outing, something to help him relax and take his mind off the day's grim events. With dry humour, she chose an outing to the Catacombs, the bizarre repository of the bones of millions of Parisians.

The limestone rock beneath Paris is crisscrossed with a network of quarried-out underground tunnels extending clear across the city. In 1786 the cemeteries of Paris were filled to overflowing, unable to accommodate the need, and a decision was made to utilise some of this space to accommodate the overflow. In a massive exercise lasting several months, the skeletons of the dead Parisians were moved, in unmarked wagons at the dead of night from the overcrowded cemeteries to an area of the catacombs near Place Denfert-Rochereau. Today, the place is open to the public to visit.

After the confrontation on Île Saint-Louis, Kon and I walked across the Pont Saint-Louis. Halfway across, we stopped and leaned on the parapet admiring the view.

"What now?" asked Kon.

I thought for a minute. "Let's put ourselves in the shoes of the opposition. Until now they were operating in secrecy but now they know that there is someone looking for them. How would you react if you were them?"

"I'd speed things up, try and get the job done before anyone could ruin my plan."

"I agree. But there's also a more aggressive response. They could turn around and eliminate the threat."

"Meaning you and me?"

"And Tisch and Mimi and Kathy and Ron."

"You think we're all at risk?" asked Kon.

"I do think that."

"What can we do about it?"

"Be very careful."

"Can you be more specific?"

"I think we – you and I – should basically act as body-guards for the rest of the group," I said. "We are the most able-bodied on our side. The others are either older, like Carlton, or female, like Mimi and Kathy."

"What about Ron Halfshaft?"

"He's younger but he's also pretty flaky. I have doubts about his ability to defend himself."

Kon nodded. "Makes sense. How do you want to organise all that? We should have a plan."

I nodded. "Why don't you take care of the situation at the Hôtel des Saints-Pères and I will keep an eye on Carlton and Mimi at the Meurice."

He nodded. "Got it."

· · ·

I returned to the Meurice and checked in at the Presidential suite.

Mimi was there.

"What's new?" I asked.

"Carlton will be back in a minute. We're going to the Catacombs."

"To look at thousands of bleached bones? How cheerful."

"Yeah," she grinned. "But I've never seen them and one needs some light relief once in a while. Why not come along?"

There was nothing I could do just then to advance the search for Zidane, so why not? A taxi was ordered.

I had to credit Mimi for a good idea. She did an excellent job of humanising Carlton. He was naturally intense and at times like this she stopped him from getting too wound up.

Mimi had started out as a Playboy bunny. It was a legitimate career but one for which the qualifications were mainly physical – there were probably still a few tattered copies around of an old August issue featuring a full frontal Mimi smiling enticingly at the world.

However, she had a shrewd brunette head on her shoulders and she had adjusted smoothly to life as the consort of a New York billionaire.

When Carlton invited her to become his third wife, she must have wondered how things would go. There is said to be a prenup slanted strongly in her favour. But somehow things had clicked, perhaps because they shared a dry sense of humour. She could still debunk pretension with a brief one liner in a Yorkshire accent undiluted by American exposure.

"Let's go," said Tisch in the lobby. He paused. "I just need to fetch something from the room. Oliver, come with me. Mimi, wait here, we'll be right back."

In the bedroom, he crossed to a bureau and opened the top drawer. He took out not one but two identical automatic pistols and handed one to me. I recognised a Beretta 9 millimetre.

"Put this in your pocket," he said. "Take care, it's loaded."

I shook my head. "How in the world did you get these into the country?"

"I didn't. Goldhawk got them for me. It pays to have resourceful friends. I actually got three of them. I gave one to Kon."

"I had no idea you were so bloodthirsty."

"I'm not, but I like a fair fight and you can be sure Zidane and Mifuba won't be relying on just words to make their point."

I slipped the Beretta into my pocket and we set out.

The taxi deposited us at Place Denfert-Rochereau

Above the entrance to the Catacombs were engraved the words:

"Arrête! C'est ici l'empire de la Mort."
(*Stop! This is the Empire of the Dead.*)

"Charming," said Tisch. We paid and entered.

We descended a narrow staircase that took us 20 metres underground before stepping out onto level ground in the shape of a dark passageway. After some yards it led to a gallery where a macabre array of skulls, scoured by age to a white matt finish, grinned at us in the gloom.

There were not many other visitors around. Unlike Oliver, Tisch and Mimi had rented self-guiding gadgets that hung around their necks. They were listening to the commentary through headsets when, out of the corner of his eye, Tisch saw another figure come around the corner. He had never seen Fredy before but this was a dark skinned African carrying a gun. Not a huge stretch to guess that it was Fredy.

Cursing his own carelessness, Tisch put an arm around Mimi's shoulders and tried to shepherd her towards the exit but Fredy was there, heading them off.

Tisch glanced around desperately. The only other option was to go deeper into the Catacombs, so he was forced to do so. Here the tunnels were darker and less well-kept, long passages stretching into the darkness.

There was a gateway on the right that Tisch could have used as an exit, avoiding Fredy, but it was old, with an iron gate secured by a rusty padlock and clearly not meant for casual visitors. Tisch drew his Beretta – he was not an experienced marksman and handled it gingerly – and used it to put a bullet in the padlock. The sound of the shot echoed hollowly through the catacombs and the gate swung open with a creak. He slipped quickly through the gate pulling Mimi with him.

They walked a few more steps until the darkness was total. They held hands and stood as quiet as possible, not daring to move. Silence reigned.

They dared to hope that Fredy had passed by and was searching in a different area.

"Are you okay?" Mimi whispered.

"Yes, but how the hell will we get out of here? I can't see a thing!"

"Hold on." Mimi reached for her mobile phone. She clicked it on and the screen lit up. With their eyes accustomed to the darkness it was like night and day. They could see their way back to the gate. Walking as quietly as they could, they covered the fifty feet at good speed and were about to exit the tunnel when:

"Sorry my friends, that's as far as you go."

Fredy stepped out of an alcove, his gun trained on Mimi at a distance of six feet. She and Tisch stopped dead.

Tisch was holding his Beretta loosely by his side. He briefly considered trying to use it but there was no time. Mifuba clearly held the advantage.

There was a quick duel of wits between Fredy and Mimi as she instinctively switched off her phone, blacking out the lighted screen. But Fredy was not taken by surprise; he had his own phone in his left hand and switched it on just as she switched hers off, so the dim but adequate light was uninterrupted.

"What now?" said Tisch.

"As I said, this is as far as you go," said Fredy.

The negotiator in Tisch kicked in. "What exactly do you want? Maybe we can give it to you."

Fredy smiled. "That's unlikely."

"I've been in business a long time," said Tisch, "And I've learned one thing. Everyone has his price."

"You're right," said Fredy. "But mine is not measured in terms of money."

"What then?"

"It's measured in lives."

"That's crazy," said Tisch.

"I am a little crazy. Hadn't you heard?" said Fredy.

"Do you really know just what your friend Zidane is planning?"

"Yes, I do."

"A nuclear explosion?"

"A small one."

Tisch forced himself to speak calmly. "How will killing us help you?"

Fredy shook his head. "I'm not stupid. Clearly if I let you live you will move heaven and earth to stop Zidane. I can't take the chance."

"Do you really think that, if you kill us, you can get out of here safely?"

"Actually I do. These limestone walls muffle the sound of gunshots quite effectively. And this section of tunnel is seldom used. Your bodies could lie here for weeks or even months before anybody notices.

He waved his gun away from Mimi and towards Tisch, then back again.

"As a courtesy, I will let you decide who I shoot first, Mr. Tisch. You, or the lady?"

"That would depend," said Tisch. Where the hell was Oliver?

"On what?"

"It's a matter of estate planning." He was really playing for time now.

Fredy blinked. What was the man talking about?

"You see, if I die first, most of my estate goes to Mimi. Then it will follow on to her family and various young folk in the north of England. On the other hand, if Mimi dies first, most of my estate goes to a range of U.S. charities." He smiled at Fredy. "Would you like to know which charities?"

Fredy shook his head. He had cottoned on to the fact that Tisch was just buying time. He raised his gun at the American – deal with him first, he was the greater threat – then finish the woman. His finger tightened on the trigger.

The shot that rang out was deafening.

I cursed my inattention. It had taken me too long to notice that Tisch and Mimi were missing. It was pure luck that I noticed the broken lock on the rusty iron gate, and spotted the dim light from Fredy's phone. I rushed after them into the dark passage but it was impossible to get an accurate shot in the dim light. Seeing how desperate things were, I fired at Fredy's outline.

He cursed but evidently the wound was far from fatal. He cancelled his phone before I could take another shot, plunging the area into darkness.

I felt the breeze as he passed within inches of me. He must have scoped out his path before killing the light.

Mimi's phone had fallen to the ground. She scrabbled around and finally found it, but by the time she could cast light on the scene, Fredy was gone.

We made our way cautiously to the exit and the light of day.

"Well we're all still here," said Tisch.

"By the skin of our teeth," said Mimi drily. "That man means business."

Tisch nodded. "Now we know what to expect."

"It's kill or be killed," I said.

It sounded dramatic, but the silence of the others acknowledged that it was true.

Back at the Neuilly house, Fredy inspected his arm which had been grazed by Oliver's bullet. It was painful but not serious. He searched the medicine cupboard in the bathroom and found iodine and bandages. He cleaned the wound, wincing as the iodine did its work, and bound it up.

He was quietly furious because he had wasted an opportunity to eliminate the key threat to his plan. Now his opponents would be warier and his task twice as difficult. But he had gone too far to turn back. He must accelerate his plans – forward was the only way.

He called Zidane.

"What's happening?" asked the Algerian.

"We must move fast," said Fredy. He described the events of the afternoon.

Zidane listened in silence. Finally, he said, "Things are moving ahead. The device will be in Paris shortly."

"How shortly?"

"In a few days."

"What's the status of the two million I gave you?" Fredy asked.

"It has been utilised," said Zidane." He said nothing about the $400,000 commission he had set aside for himself.

Fredy did not pursue the subject He had entrusted a great deal of money to the Algerian who he had only known for a short time. If it was misused, he would have little recourse. It was a risk. But he could afford it and his judgment was that the funds would essentially be used for their stated purpose.

He rang off. What about his next step? Nobody outside the office of the lawyer Hannay knew where he was living now, so he would have the advantage of surprise if he launched another attack on Tisch and his friends.

41

I was very uneasy about the looming threat posed by Fredy Mifuba. He was a potentially lethal loose end and we had no idea where he was.

What should I do about the safety of Carlton and Mimi? I could send Kon to keep an eye on them but that would leave Ron Halfshaft unprotected. It was a tough choice. I did not have enough manpower.

I suddenly thought of Harry Hodge, the man I had played squash with. Here was a former commando and boxer with a squash player's reflexes, a boarding school and Oxbridge product at a loose end in Paris. Except for the drinking he checked all the boxes. And I didn't have a lot of options. I picked up the phone.

"Hello?"

Good, he sounded sober. "It's Oliver Steele. We played squash the other day."

"I remember. I should have beaten you."

"Next time."

"Of course. What's up?"

I took a deep breath. "You won't believe this, but ..."

The upshot was that I recruited Harry Hodge to go the Meurice and keep an eye on Tisch and Mimi. I gave him my pistol. Kon Feaver would remain at the Saints-Pères hotel and hang out with Ron Halfshaft. I suppose subconsciously I considered Ron the more vulnerable target. It was not a scientific judgment but I had known Tisch longer and had considerable respect for his resourcefulness in an emergency. I had nothing against Ron but there wasn't the same level of confidence.

I talked to Kon. I wanted to be sure that he had one of Tisch's Berettas. It was a weapon with which he was familiar and I knew he was comfortable with a gun in his hand. He was an excellent marksman and he had plenty of experience. After being kicked out of the Israeli Air Force and then getting sober he had bounced around the world in a series of brief careers. In Africa he enlisted as a mercenary in an abortive attempt to invade Equatorial Guinea and overthrow the fearsome President Teodoro Obiang. That coup turned into a farce when the Boeing 727 carrying the mercenaries was arrested in Zimbabwe just before take off.

He managed to squeak out of that situation and moved to Miami. There he dealt marijuana from a house in Coconut Grove. It seemed a good idea at the time but turned out to be such a sleazy game that he quit after a month, donating his remaining inventory to some of his friends. That was when he started running boatloads of Cuban fugitives from Havana to Miami.

"You still have the gun Tisch gave you, don't you?" I asked

He nodded, patting his pocket. He pulled it out, checked that the clip was full, fifteen rounds, and nodded. "Extra clip?"

"Sorry, don't have," I said. "Make them count."

He grinned.

There was nothing more I could do. Sometimes one gets the feeling that things are slipping out of control. I had that feeling now. Well, I was doing my best with limited resources.

42

F redy was mortified. He knew he must learn from his clumsy mistake in the Catacombs. He had failed to deal with Tisch and his party and the incident almost cost him his life.

He was outnumbered, but that could be fixed.

He made a phone call to Kongolo.

Jules, the President's bodyguard answered on the first ring. Kongolo was 3,000 miles south of Paris but it was in a time zone only one hour ahead, so it was morning in both places.

He was in his apartment watching American football on the Sports Channel. Kongolo City enjoyed excellent TV reception thanks to the powerful antenna less than a hundred yards from the palace that enabled the President to indulge his love of American soap operas, which he watched for several hours a day.

"Monsieur Fredy, how are you?"

"Fine Jules, how are you?"

"Very well, Sir. A pleasure to hear from you."

The burly bodyguard was never sure how to treat Fredy. He had to show respect but he could not use the easy manner that he employed with the President. That was something special, akin to the relationship between officer and sergeant in wartime, a rapport rooted in shared danger. The President's supremacy might seem effortless to outsiders but he had faced many rivals over the years – from populists seeking democracy to cynical generals interested only in grabbing power for themselves – and many times Jules had paid a late night call on an unsuspecting officer or a Senator who mistakenly believed that his title really meant something. A single shot usually took care of matters, although Jules could be just as deadly with a sharp knife.

So lacking the same rapport with the son he was tentative. "How can I help?"

"I have a job for you."

"Wet or dry?" It was a well understood shorthand.

"Wet."

"Where will that be?"

"Here in France."

"You wish me to come to Paris?"

"Yes, immediately."

Jules was up for that. He liked to travel and he had

been to Paris several times, living high on the hog, buying women and eating in the best restaurants.

So he had no problem with flying to France or with carrying out an execution when he got there. The law in foreign jurisdictions meant nothing to him. He certainly did not fear it. But he wondered what the President would think of Fredy's activity. He was aware of the confiscation of the Paris mansion and from what he knew of Fredy there was probably some kind of revenge plan in the works.

He was concerned about that – it would be characteristic of Fredy to want to do something violent against the former colonial power as retribution for being thrown out of his home.

So he thought he had better clear things with the President.

But he wanted to appear positive to Fredy so he said, "Of course. Is the plane available?"

"No it's here in Paris, and time is of the essence. You'll have to take public transport."

"Very well. The daily Air Maroc flight to Casablanca leaves in a few hours and it connects with an Air France flight to Paris. I can probably be with you late tonight."

"Rent a car at the airport," said Fredy. He gave Jules the address in Neuilly. "Get one with a satnav. You can sleep here."

.   .   .

Jules did not head straight for the airport. In Kongolo things were not that simple. He left his apartment downtown and drove in his white Range Rover the five miles to the presidential palace. The sleek vehicle contrasted jarringly with the dusty streets in need of repair and row upon row of poor hovels but that did not bother Jules. He had grown used to the elevated standard of living that was the privilege of the President's inner circle.

He parked in the forecourt, nodded at the armed sentries in sweat-stained fatigues standing guard, and strolled into the palace.

Inside, his progress was checked by Dikembe, chief steward and secretary to the President. Next to Jules, Dikembe was the man the President trusted most. Tall and frowning, he was the President's gatekeeper. If you wanted to speak to the President you had go through Dikembe. Jules knew this and did not try to short circuit the system.

"Is he in?"

"That depends what you want," said Dikembe.

He and Jules were old sparring partners in terms of competing for the President's ear. Jules thought Dikembe was obsequious and political, which he was. Dikembe on the other hand, had watched Jules curry favour over the years and although he thought him crude and unsubtle he could see that they were on a par when it came to influence. So, although they disliked each other, there was an understanding.

"Fredy wants me in Paris. I would like to clear it with the President first."

Dikembe nodded. He would have done the same in Jules's place.

"I'll see if he's available."

A few minutes later Jules stood respectfully in front of the President who was reading the 'National Enquirer' – he had a selection of trashy U.S. papers flown in every week.

"What is it?" Mifuba grumbled. He looked tired, thought Jules. Seventy was not a great age but life spans were short in that part of the world and Mifuba had led an eventful life. He had surgery for prostate cancer the year before. He claimed to be fully recovered but Jules though it had taken some of the energy out of him.

"I had a call from Monsieur Fredy," said Jules.

"Oh?"

"He wants me in Paris as soon as possible."

"To do what?"

"I'm not sure. But I assume it has something to do with the confiscation of the house on Victor Hugo."

"Oh yes." The President had mixed feelings about that. He was angry – and with him that entailed seeking revenge – but he did not share his son's feeling of violation. The place was too remote to affect him in that way. He assumed that Fredy wanted Jules to shoot someone, which was okay. It was what Jules was for.

He looked at Jules appraisingly.

"How many people have you killed, young man?"

"About twelve."

"About? Don't you keep count?"

"A figure of speech. It's exactly twelve. Thirteen if you

include the guy who died after I knocked him out in the boxing ring. I felt bad about that."

"You felt bad?"

"Yes, because it was a mistake. I don't like mistakes."

The older man nodded sympathetically. "Neither do I. Well I suppose it's all right. Try to discourage my son from doing anything really stupid."

Jules laughed. "I understand."

Neither of them knew what Fredy was planning. If the President had any idea, he would certainly have vetoed it. He had enough political sense to know that no good could come of it for him or for Kongolo, that it would make them international pariahs. There was enough bad publicity already without something like that.

Jules did not check any baggage. He had packed a light grip with a few clean shirts and some socks and underwear. He carried no weapons. He would deal with that when he arrived. No books either. Jules was not a reader.

On the plane he watched movies and dozed. It was dark when he landed at Charles de Gaulle and drove through the Paris suburbs in his rented car, keeping an eye on the colourful navigation screen and obeying the French spoken commands. He arrived at the house in Neuilly around 2 a.m. and rang the bell.

Fredy opened the door and saw Jules standing on the doorstep. Fredy gave a little bow. "Good evening, or should I say good morning."

They shook hands. They were both athletic and were similar in height but Jules was much the more powerful, his broad chest and muscular arms straining the dark cotton suit he had chosen for this expedition.

They eyed each other cautiously. They had never been friendly but had a mutual respect based on each other's strengths and their places in Kongolo's political structure.

Jules was there because he was useful to the President, while Fredy was there by right of birth. But each man knew that with a President as capricious as Francois Mifuba, things could change in a heartbeat. There had been other bodyguards, crude fellows who had said something out of turn and were no longer around. And a few dead relatives of the President including the uncle he had executed in succeeding to the presidency were a grim reminder that even blood was not everything, thought Fredy.

He showed Jules to a bedroom. "Get settled in, then come and have a drink and we'll talk."

When they were seated in armchairs, each with a glass in his hand, Fredy said, "You probably know that our country is under financial attack."

Nice choice of words, thought Jules. Like everyone in Kongolo he knew about the fire in the refinery and that it would be closed for a year. That sort of information flashed through the grapevine in minutes. So did word of the confiscation of the Victor Hugo house. European news might be sparse in Kongolo but you couldn't prevent a disgruntled staff of twenty people from spreading the word. So now everyone who mattered in Kongolo knew exactly what was going on. But unless it affected their daily lives, like the refinery workers, most people just shrugged and carried on. There had been plenty of political turmoil over the years and people knew that it didn't pay to have opinions, let alone express them.

So Jules just nodded and waited for Fredy to go on.

"Some people have been giving me trouble," said Fredy. "They could cost me a lot of money."

"Something to do with the so-called money-laundering? A disgraceful attack on our country!" Jules had no idea if that was true but it was a safe remark.

Fredy nodded. He was pleased. This was going to work out. Jules would not ask for any details. There was no need even to mention Zidane or the Pakistan connection.

Jules knew he was not hearing the whole story but he did not mind. Things were simpler that way. "So who are these people? Where do they hang out?"

"There are six of them." Fredy counted off on his fingers. "The American Tisch, his wife Mimi and his wife's friend Kathy. Those are staying at the Hotel Meurice on Rue de Rivoli.

"Then there is a group at the Hotel des Saints-Pères on the Left Bank. As well as a Britisher called Steele and an Israeli, name of Kon Feaver, it includes, according to my sources, an American computer expert called Halfshaft."

"Your sources?"

"Our French attorney Fabrice Hannay sent a detective to look around and see who was involved."

"Which individuals need removing?"

"All of them."

Jules raised an eyebrow. He had not expected to have to kill six people. Not that he had any moral scruples but it sounded as if the task would take a bit of planning.

Fredy noticed Jules's surprise. He said, "The group at the Meurice will be particularly on the alert." He described the incident in the Catacombs, slanting the facts so as to reflect the least discredit on himself. "So we must start with the others, the ones at the Saints-Pères."

"Have you met any of them?"

"Personally? Yes, Feaver and the Britisher."

"What are they like?"

Fredy frowned, recalling the incident in the Île Saint-Louis apartment. What with the unintended death of Katerina and the ensuing firefight, it had not gone well. But he was reluctant to admit that Feaver and Steele had shown superior mettle. He put their success down to sheer luck.

"Not pushovers," he said finally. "But not in your league," he added in a clumsy compliment.

Jules brushed that off. He was fully confident of his own ability and considered flattery irrelevant. "Are they armed?"

"Yes."

"What do we have in the way of guns?"

Fredy stood up and, beckoning Jules, walked into his bedroom. He pulled open the bottom drawer of the heavy mahogany dresser. Inside were two firearms, each wrapped in chamois leather.

Jules nodded approval. He was a collector and enthusiast with a large selection of guns at home in Kongolo and recognised both weapons.

One was a Sig Sauer MCX, a semi-automatic rifle with a magazine capacity of thirty rounds. Jules had seen it described in catalogues as a modern sporting rifle which in his opinion was a joke – there was nothing sporting about it, it was for killing people. The other was a Glock 17, a nine millimeter semi-automatic pistol with a seventeen round magazine.

Jules liked the semi-automatic format. It required the user to pull the trigger for each shot, unlike a full automatic where one pull would keep the weapon firing until the magazine was exhausted. Like many users he found an automatic difficult to control while it was emitting a steady stream of bullets. In his experience a semi-automatic was much more effective.

He had not killed anyone with a Glock, preferring the better balanced Beretta but he had often practised with it. The American gun lobby liked to insist that such weapons were not automatic but they were quite fast enough for him. He could discharge a full magazine accurately in under four seconds.

"These will do. Where did you get them?"

Fredy smiled. "My attorney is very resourceful."

Jules looked at his watch. "First thing tomorrow, we go to that hotel and scope things out?"

"That's the plan."

"One more thing," said Jules. He strolled into the kitchen.

"What are you looking for?" asked Fredy.

"I just found it." There was a solid wooden butcher's block on the counter containing an array of kitchen knives. He pulled out several, testing them with his finger and selected one with a narrow, razor-sharp blade six inches long. He wrapped a folded paper towel round the blade and slipped it into his jacket pocket.

"Now I shall sleep well."

Hodge took a taxi to the Meurice and introduced himself to Tisch.

The financier had just been jogging and was looking his age. He wore an old tracksuit and looked in need of a shower. Hodge took that in. He himself was more formal. The army years were stamped on his dress – twill trousers, suede shoes and an expensive made to measure tweed jacket. It was cut to be worn with one button fastened but its line would have been spoiled by the Beretta and holster at his shoulder so instead he wore it loose. He only needed a regimental tie and a Viyella shirt with tiny checks to be the model off-duty officer but, as a concession to informality, he sported a pink Ralph Lauren polo shirt and no tie.

"Oliver said you would drop by. I'm not sure why, but welcome anyway," said Carlton.

"I'm a kind of security assistant," said Hodge. He had

taken careful thought and decided to avoid the word bodyguard.

"Is that necessary?"

"Oliver seems to think so. On account of some bad people around."

"Better safe than sorry I suppose," said Tisch without enthusiasm.

"That's a really nice jacket," said Mimi.

Fredy and Jules drove into town. Jules sat in the passenger seat of the Lexus, looking out at the spacious houses and well kept streets of Neuilly.

He didn't know what lay in store. That itself was exciting. It would be dangerous but never mind, he was going to enjoy himself. Something primitive stirred in his soul, the thrill of the chase. It warmed the blood.

But he must think things through. There had to be a plan. You didn't gun down several people on the street in broad daylight and just walk casually away. It bothered him that Fredy had said nothing about what would happen afterwards. Clearly it was up to Jules to develop a strategy and then execute it.

"How many entrances does the hotel have?"

Fredy shook his head. "I have no idea."

"Have you been there?"

"No," said Fredy shortly. He didn't like being cross-examined by an underling.

"Okay," said Jules. "We start by driving the area. Past the

hotel and round the block. See which streets are quiet and which are busy. Where one could fire a gun and not have it heard."

"And then what?"

"That'll do for starters."

There was something about the way Jules spoke that made Fredy take his eyes off the road for a moment and look at Jules. The bodyguard took no notice.

"Don't forget who you work for," said Fredy.

"I work for your father," said Jules coldly. "Find a quiet spot and stop the car. I need to do some things before we reach the city."

In a secluded turning off the country road, Jules opened the trunk and took out the Glock and the Sig Sauer rifle. He put both weapons on the floor in the back of the car. Before leaving the house he had checked the action of the Glock and had stripped down and reassembled the rifle and tested its mechanism until he was happy that both weapons worked perfectly. The last thing he wanted was a jam or misfire at a key moment.

He looked around for a suitable mud puddle. Finding one, he dipped a towel in it and smeared mud over both the car's license plates. He stood back and admired his handiwork. After a couple of careful retouches the numbers were completely obscured.

His plan was to lie in wait in the car until, sooner or later, Halfshaft left the hotel. Then the Lexus would follow the Californian. When an opportunity arose Jules would let loose with a burst of rifle fire.

That was the easy part. They then had to escape and the Lexus would be the way to do it. Bystanders might or might not be alert enough to look for the car's license number but it wouldn't matter how observant they were if the plates were unreadable.

Satisfied with his handiwork, Jules got back in the car and nodded at Fredy. "Let's go into town."

Ron Halfshaft had been wondering how to make good use of the information he had downloaded from Fredy Mifuba's mobile phone. He had turned it over to Solly Goldhawk's programmers to analyse but he had a feeling they would not come up with much that would be useful. He suspected they had bled that vein dry.

But he now knew the basic signature of Fredy's phone and there were a couple of tricks he wanted to try. After breakfast he went back to his room and plugged in the book-sized device he had used to capture Fredy's data. He linked it to his own phone, a Samsung Galaxy, and pressed a series of keys.

A map of Paris appeared, jewel-like on the Samsung's high-resolution screen. It closely resembled a map from the taxi company Uber. Subscribers to Uber see little moving icons representing Uber cabs that are in their vicinity and can tell how close is the nearest one. Ron had been fascinated by the system when it first came out. But unlike most people who just regarded Uber as a useful resource, he regarded it as a challenge, something to be copied, analysed and – why not? – improved on.

So while other visitors might spend the morning seeing the sights of Paris or planning where to have dinner, Ron spent a happy few hours tinkering, punctuated by calls down to the kitchen for refills of the hotel's excellent filter coffee. When he finally stood up to stretch his legs it was with a definite feeling of achievement.

Kon walked through the door of the Hotel des Saints-Pères at lunchtime and telephoned Ron's room. Moments later the Californian appeared.

"Hi!"

What's up?" asked Halfshaft. He was wearing a T-shirt and jeans. His face was its usual indoor white and he had not shaved.

"Fredy Mifuba may be gunning for you," said Kon.

Ron smiled. "I know."

He's very confident, thought Kon. "Aren't you concerned?"

"Not really. I'm not saying I'm a hero, I'm a lover, not a fighter. But I reckon I'll see him coming and take evasive action. That's more my style."

"I'm glad to hear it," said Kon. He wasn't sure what Ron meant. "It never hurts to be prepared."

Ron shrugged. "Exactly."

Kon scanned the lobby. "I'm going to take a look

around. This is an old building. I still haven't figured out the layout."

"Knock yourself out. I'll be upstairs programming. Hammer on the door when you're done."

Kon strolled round the ground floor noting the location of the bar and dining room, the toilets and a door leading to the kitchens. As he watched, a waiter emerged carrying a tray and boarded the guest lift to the higher floors. Was there no separate service lift? It was not a purpose-built hotel, so that was possible. A rear exit led to the street behind the hotel and another exit was marked for use only in case of fire. He took all this in and then walked up to Ron's room by the old stone staircase.

The Californian stood up, running his hands through his hair. "I'm ready for some fresh air."

"What are you working on?"

"It's a new app I came up with, designed to run on mobile phones."

"What does it do?"

"Are you familiar with Uber?"

"No."

"It's a programme that lets you order a taxi from your mobile phone."

"Okay."

"I'm adapting it so that you can look on your phone and see the whereabouts of another caller."

"Is that useful?"

Ron was nonplussed for a moment. "It's a really cool programme," he said defensively.

"How does it work?"

"It's done by triangulating between phone towers."

"New technology?"

Ron shook his head. "It's been around for a while. The police use it. What's new is the way I hacked into a police mainframe to get the software." He grinned. "Want to know something?"

"What?"

"It works even when the phone's owner is not calling. Just as long as his phone is switched on."

Kon was polite. "That's wonderful."

The Lexus carrying Fredy and Jules reached the centre of Paris and Fredy asked, "Where now?"

"Saint-Germain-des-Prés. Drive past the hotel."

Approaching via the Boulevard Saint-Germain they turned north onto Rue des Saints-Pères and drove slowly past the hotel. It was much less grand than the Meurice, but it was a respectable bourgeois establishment in a street of grey stone townhouses with its name engraved in Roman lettering above the entrance.

There was nothing about the Lexus to attract attention and their progress was uneventful. At the end of Rue des Saints-Pères they turned right onto Quai Malaquais and drove east alongside the Seine for half a mile before turning right down Rue Guénégaud, and then back onto Rue des Saints-Pères. This time they stopped by the kerb twenty yards short of the hotel and settled down to wait.

. . .

"**Where shall we walk?**" asked Kon.

"We?"

"Where you go, I go."

"Let's go and check out the Bouquinistes."

"And what might those be?"

As usual, Ron surprised with his knowledge. "They are the dealers in used and antiquarian books who sell from stalls alongside the Seine."

Kon had nothing better to do. "Sure. Where exactly do they hang out?"

Ron said, "We turn right out of the hotel, go along Rue des Saints-Pères for 150 yards, cross over Rue de L'Université, go another 100 yards, then turn left onto Rue de Vermeuil. Go straight for 150 yards then make a right onto Rue de Beaune. After 200 more yards we'll hit Quai Voltaire, by the river. Turn right and there they are."

Kon blinked. "Are you sure about those yardages?" he asked sarcastically.

"Quite sure," said Ron. He paused. "I have this memory thing. I look at the map and it's in here." He tapped his skull.

His measurements were accurate within a few feet. Minutes later they were browsing among old first editions, water-colour prints of Paris and a selection of junk aimed at tourists.

As they strolled Kon asked, "What did you mean when you said you could see the bad guys coming?"

Ron took out his mobile phone and clicked it. "I can use my new app." He showed Kon the gleaming screen.

"What's that red dot moving across the map?" Kon asked.

"That shouldn't be there," said Ron. He looked surprised. "I thought I had it debugged but apparently not. That would mean Fredy Mifuba – or his mobile phone – was only twenty yards away."

Kon swung round and looked back down the Quai Voltaire. "Your app may be smarter than you thought."

He swept an arm across Ron's chest and threw him to the ground, following himself. In a second they both lay flat on the concrete.

His quick thinking saved their lives. The silver Lexus that had been rolling along behind, tracking them, accelerated with a roar. A rapid burst of fire spat from the rifle sticking out of the window.

Fredy wrestled the Lexus in an effort to get closer. His enthusiasm caused the car's right hand wheels to mount the pavement. The jolt distracted Jules at the crucial moment. He could not correct his aim and although he pulled the trigger Ron and Kon were unharmed.

Others were less lucky. An elderly bystander in a beret – a bookseller or perhaps a browser – took a bullet in the face and collapsed on the concrete. A young woman in jeans who looked like a tourist was also hit. She did not go down but doubled over and clutched her arm, screaming. Bullets tore through the open book boxes lining the embankment, sending a shower of books, prints and papers flying into the air.

Amid the chaos, the Lexus bumped off the pavement and back onto the road.

Jules, livid with anger, shouted, " Get out of sight. Take a side street."

Trying to comply, Fredy swerved across the yellow line in the middle of the road and hit the fender of a Mercedes van. The van was unharmed but the left front wing of the Lexus was ripped away and a cloud of steam shot from its radiator. Fredy pumped the accelerator and the Lexus limped along, but at a fraction of its normal pace.

Ron and Kon got to their feet. Ron, dazed, had some vague idea that he should photograph the chaos. He fiddled with his camera. Kon was more concerned with tracking the Lexus which was a hundred yards away along Quai Voltaire and turning onto Rue de Seine.

"What about the wounded?" Ron muttered.

Kon shook his head. "Never mind that. We have to track those bastards."

They hurried to the corner and looked down Rue de Seine but the street was empty. Apparently Jules's getaway had succeeded.

Kon turned to Ron. "Now would be a good time to use your app. Where are they?"

Ron fumbled with the keys and managed to get the right screen. They pored over it. The little red dot was stationary. It was positioned not on a street but in a building around a corner several blocks away.

"How accurate is that thing?" Kon asked.

"Plus or minus ten feet."

"So if the red dot is off the road, then so is Fredy?"

"Probably."

As they approached the final turn before the red dot's location, Kon drew his Beretta. Rounding the corner they half expected to see the Lexus and there it stood, sad and damaged, by the kerb. It had finally died. Steam rose from the radiator and oil puddled on the ground below.

Rue du Général Olivier Cointre was narrow like many of the maze of streets in the area between Boulevard Saint-Germain and the Seine and there seemed to be nobody about.

"Where's the dot now? Check again," said Kon.

"It hasn't moved," said Ron. "No wait, I think it's a bit further off road. Maybe not. The scale is so small it's hard to tell."

"You need to refine the technology," said Kon.

Ron was indignant. "It's state of the art, give me a break." His sense of humour was hit-and-miss sometimes.

The street consisted of a mixture of residential units with garages and warehouses. Kon guessed that their quarry, forced to abandon the Lexus, had tried to open any door they could find in order to get out of sight. In their shoes he would have got as far as possible from the tell tale car. It was a reasonable plan except that the Kongolans had not allowed for Ron's red dot.

He took a last look at the screen. The dot had not

moved. It still placed Fredy in a building a hundred yards from the car. They approached cautiously.

It was a windowless warehouse. There was a metal roll-up gate twelve feet across, wide enough for a decent sized truck. At one side was a grey wooden door. Gun in hand, Kon tried the door gently. It was unlocked. Parisians, like most folk in big cities, are not known for their trusting nature and tend to lock their doors so Fredy must have felt it was his lucky day, Kon thought.

He pushed the door open, standing aside so as not to present a target, and squinted through. It was a long warehouse with a twenty foot high corrugated ceiling stretching all the way back to an open area with a parked truck. Packing cases were piled high to left and right suggesting an active commercial operation. Only one thing was missing – people.

Which did not mean they weren't there, Kon thought. To find out, he would have to go in.

It was a moment of truth. He motioned to Ron to stay in the street. Muttering a quick prayer to any god that might be listening he darted inside and dived for cover behind a ten foot stack of crates. He flattened himself against the wall.

A shot rang out, followed immediately by a stream of rapid fire with a different note. Bullets ripped into the packing cases above his head. With all the echoes rattling round the tin-roofed structure, the shots could have come from any direction. But he could tell that multiple weapons were involved. That made the odds worse.

Silence followed. Kon thought about calling out. They already knew where he was. But he decided to stay quiet, listen for movement and try to get an idea of their plans. He looked at the Beretta in his hand. A nice weapon but only 15 rounds in the clip.

Analyze, he told himself. By now the street of booksellers would be teeming with police. At any minute the wrecked Lexus would probably be spotted. That meant Fredy and company would be desperate to leave the area fast. So time was on his side. He settled down to wait.

It didn't take long. The call came from a distant corner of the warehouse.

"Are you listening, American?"

Kon recognised the voice. It was Fredy, the man who had stood on Katerina's balcony and watched while Zidane beat him up.

"It's Israeli, not American. But yes, I'm listening."

"We're coming out. If you try to stop us we shall shoot you."

"Give it your best try, my friend!"

"We have more firepower."

Kon laughed. "I shoot straighter."

"Don't be so sure. My colleague is an excellent shot."

"Who is your colleague?"

"Not important. But he is a professional."

"Not like you then." Kon was baiting Fredy, keeping the dialogue going. He had the Kongolan pinpointed but what about his companion? Whoever he was, he could handle a rifle. "I tell you what. If you come out with your hands up, we can have a nice civilised discussion."

"About what?"

"Terrorism, bombs, stuff like that."

"You may have a point," said Fredy. "It's time to talk. We'll come out peacefully."

Oh right, thought Kon.

"I'm coming out now," said Fredy. "I have a pistol but look, I'll hold it by the barrel."

He stepped slowly from behind a pile of crates thirty feet away. Within Beretta range. He held up the pistol just as he promised and walked towards Kon, smiling.

Kon didn't like the smile. There was something about it.

Fredy paused when he was about ten feet from Kon.

A second figure appeared from behind the same crates, rifle at his side but this time not holding the weapon by the barrel. The business end was towards Kon, and was being raised. Kon's view was partly obscured by Fredy standing between them.

Kon's brain shifted up a gear. The next half second would be interesting. Fredy might be his new best pal. Then again he might be a human screen who would move smartly aside to give his colleague a clear shot at Kon. Hard to know which, impossible in fact.

He soon found out because a burst of rifle fire cut Fredy in half.

Human screen had been the right call but the means of its removal came as a shock. Kon had been sure something was fishy so he was ready and fired two rounds in quick succession. The range was too great to justify a headshot so he went for body mass. He wasn't sure what part of the body he hit but the man dropped his rifle, lurching past Kon and out of the door.

Kon kicked the rifle aside and followed him out.

The body lay on the pavement, either dead or insensible. Ron stood over it in an attitude of conquest. "I hit him," he said with pride.

"What with?"

Ron held up a hand. In it was his phone, screen smashed to pieces. The Samsung Galaxy had made its last call.

There was a post mortem over drinks at the Meurice. Everyone was there including the Britisher Hodge, who sounded disappointed at having missed the action.

"Are they both dead?" he asked.

"Fredy is, for sure," said Kon. "The other one was unconscious when we got out of there."

"I hit him pretty good," said Ron modestly.

Kon said, "He was losing blood fast."

"What if he's still alive?" asked Mimi.

Tisch shrugged. "Suppose he is. He won't be going anywhere but prison. Dozens of people saw him shoot that bookseller. A prison hospital is a lot better than he deserves."

There was a thoughtful silence.

"Okay," I said. "We can chalk up a minor victory. Fredy's death is a bad stain erased. But we still have a bigger problem!"

"You're right of course," said Tisch. "What Fredy started, Zidane intends to finish. The head of the monster lives."

43

October 5th

I n the bar of the Islamabad Club in Pakistan, a young nuclear engineer called Rashid Mirza sat and brooded about his future.

He had a thoughtful face, black hair and alert brown eyes. He was slim and fit, losing finalist in the Club's annual squash tournament. He was personable and could look forward to a promising career but right now he was angry and frustrated.

He was the manager of the applied devices section of Pakistan's nuclear research agency, but any credit for his department's success was routinely pre-empted by his boss Tariq Yahya, a charismatic engineer-politician with a flair for self-promotion.

Rumours were rife about Yahya selling secret nuclear material to other countries. A nation could join the nuclear club just by buying know-how from Pakistan, it was said, and the rumours had the ring of truth given Pakistan's widespread corruption.

Was Yahya really involved? Something about his sharp face and evasive way of speaking made people wonder. In fact, Yahya was not guilty, although he had few scruples and would not have minded. But press coverage and the media spotlight made it impossible. This made him, except when in front of a camera, sour and bad tempered, bad qualities in a boss, and his staff had to bear the brunt.

That morning, Yahya had been at his most unpleasant, shouting and hectoring everyone for perceived mistakes, none of which amounted to anything. They were just excuses for Yahya to sound off.

Finally, Mirza sought out Aziz, a close colleague.

"Let's forget that meeting, it was embarrassing. I want to talk about something else."

They both knew what he meant. It was something that Yahya, with all his noisy grandstanding, knew nothing about.

"I have been approached," said Mirza.

Aziz's eyes widened.

For about a year, the two had been quietly working on a secret project in their personal time, a miniature tactical device. It would have the explosive equivalent of half a kiloton of TNT, a small fraction of the size of the bomb dropped on Hiroshima, and could literally be carried in a suitcase. Working discreetly, they had been designing the parts, radioactive cores and circuitry required for such a device.

Now, as they had long hoped, the project might be approaching commercial reality.

"So, who called?" asked Aziz.

"Munir Chaudry, an old university friend. We met as students at Imperial College London. He's an attaché with the embassy in Paris now."

"What exactly did he want?"

Mirza thought back to his telephone conversation with Chaudry.

After some initial pleasantries, Chaudry had asked, "Do you remember telling me once that you could make an atom bomb that would fit in the overhead baggage rack of a 747?"

Mirza laughed. "I was probably drunk."

"But could you do it?"

"Yes, I could. Mind you, the kind of plane that would be used to bomb a city like Delhi or Mumbai could carry much heavier devices than that, so the weight is not really critical."

"For another purpose it might be."

"A tactical weapon, you mean, for use on the battlefield?"

"Something like that."

"As far as I know, Pakistan has no plans that would require a portable device," said Mirza disingenuously.

"I'm not talking about Pakistan."

"What, then?"

"I don't want to be specific. But I can tell you that the price is right."

Neither Chaudry nor Mirza had much money and it was a sore point. Some of their contemporaries had moved to the United States and were earning million dollar salaries as surgeons or hedge fund managers. Compared to them, Mirza and Chaudry were almost paupers, and it rankled. They had discussed ways of making money but had not come up with anything specific.

Until now.

Chaudry said, "I may have a customer."

"Customer or country?"

"An individual representing a country," said Chaudry. Mirza noted the choice of words. Was Chaudry talking about terrrorism? The terrorist state was sort of like a country.

Chaudry said, "It's not an enemy of Pakistan. Your patriotism would not be strained."

"How would I profit from this?" Mirza asked.

"I have already secured the money. There is $1.6 million in an escrow account in Liechtenstein. Half of it will be disbursed when we – you and I – agree to go ahead. The balance will be paid on delivery."

"How will *you* profit?" asked Mirza. He could be just as blunt as Chaudry.

"We split the money. Equal partners."

Mirza laughed. "That doesn't sound fair. I shall be doing the lion's share of the work."

"That's debatable. Anyway, without me there's no deal."

Mirza saw the force of that. He tried to think about the practical details.

"I shall have expenses."

"What expenses?"

"Components, the labour to assemble them. Payments to a colleague."

"Nobody other than yourself must be involved. It would be too risky." Chaudry sounded uneasy.

"It's also unavoidable, this is a two-man job, at least. And the fellow engineer I have in mind isn't stupid, he will know exactly what is going on."

"Then it must be on a 'need to know' basis."

"Of course."

"How much will your expenses be?" Chaudry asked.

Mirza thought for a moment. They might be friends but this was becoming a negotiation.

"I would need to think," he said.

"Take a guess."

"Two hundred thousand," said Mirza.

He actually had no idea. The cost would certainly not be that much. Compared to the sums Chaudry had mentioned it would be trivial. He could do much of the building work at home in his garage.

"That much?"

"It's a nuclear bomb, for goodness sake. But two hundred grand should cover it."

Chaudry said, "Here's what I suggest. We split the first $800,000, receiving $400,000 each. When it comes to the second $800,000, you again get half. In other words, you will receive $800,000 altogether. You must pay your costs, including your engineer friend, out of that."

The sheer outrageousness of what they were discussing made them fall quiet for a moment.

"Done," said Mirza.

Mirza gave Aziz an edited version of the conversation. He omitted the monetary amounts but Aziz was quick to raise the subject. "He must have offered a lot of money," he said.

"That's private. But I can tell you that your own slice of the pie, for a couple of weeks work, would equal at least three years salary at your present rate."

Mirza had thought long and hard before sharing the idea of a suitcase bomb with Aziz. The wiry Pathan, about thirty years old, came from a rural part of the Punjab. His family had lacked either the money or the sophistication to send him to study abroad but he had a degree from Lahore University of Engineering. His speciality was circuitry and switchgear. He was sharp at what he did and fitted well with Mirza's own skills.

He could communicate well on a technical level but he was otherwise quiet and unforthcoming. He was some-what of a protégé, in awe of Mirza's greater worldliness and managerial skill. Above all Mirza felt he could rely on Aziz's complete discretion.

In the weeks that followed, the project took shape.

Chaudry put Mirza in touch with the United Bank of Switzerland, where he opened a deposit account.

He chose, rather than Zurich or Basel, the picturesque town of Olten, population 18,000, with a covered wooden bridge and 15th century half-timbered houses nestling on the banks of the Aare River. A Swiss friend lived there and had often pressed him to come and visit.

Taking advantage of an engineering convention in London, he stole a vacation day, flew to Zurich and took the train to Olten, a thirty minute ride. By midday, he was sitting with his friend talking to a smiling bank manager.

The manager spoke perfect English. His name was Anton Regenschirm.

"My name means, in English, 'Umbrella.' I am the umbrella man. I protect my depositors from the rains and storms of financial adversity." He laughed heartily. He had obviously used the quip often.

Mirza signed some forms and deposited a thousand Swiss francs – just over a thousand US dollars – with the promise of more to come. Neither of the two Swiss seemed to think it surprising that he, a young Pakistani from Islamabad, should want to open an account so far away from home.

Afterwards, they all had lunch at a restaurant in the old

town – *schweinshaxe* and *rösti* washed down with a robust white wine from the Valais – and parted the best of friends. Mirza knew he could have done the whole thing by mail and telephone but he just felt better having a banker with a human face.

In due course, his first $400,000 arrived electronically. It was converted to Swiss francs and deposited in the account. On-line access enabled him to check his balance, which he did regularly.

The only drawback was that his money earned no interest but, as Herr Regenshirm cheerfully pointed out, rates were so low nowadays that it was a small price to pay for the privilege of total security.

Mirza drafted the schematics for the bomb on a drawing board in his study at home.

A portable bomb was not a new idea. During the Cold War, American Green Berets were trained to infiltrate Warsaw Pact borders carrying backpack sized nuclear bombs to blunt an attack by Soviet tanks. Mirza's office had played with variations over the years and he was able to 'cut and paste' elements of existing designs but he also added a few refinements of his own.

He made the outer housing from aluminium. Sheet metal and pressings were bolted onto a series of small castings to form the shell. He was pleased that, as a result, he was able to keep the weight to just under fifty pounds. An imitation leather covering made of vinyl was then applied.

The result was a surprisingly sleek entity that looked a bit like a Samsonite suitcase. When Mirza finally added wheelies on one corner and a telescopic handle on top, enabling the thing to be wheeled easily across a flat surface, it was identical to the other suitcases that Zidane had ordered from China and which were now in Lahore awaiting pickup.

A week before it was finished his phone rang. It was Chaudry.

"What about a game of squash?"

It was a code they had worked out. The word squash meant that things were going according to plan. If anything had been amiss, the greeting would have mentioned racquetball instead of squash. Neither message would indicate to a casual listener that anything covert was afoot.

"Where are you?" asked Mirza.

'I'm in Lahore. I thought I would see how you were getting on, and have a look at the goods."

"Is that wise?"

"Why not?"

Mirza was uneasy, but Chaudry insisted.

They were in Mirza's garage examining the almost-ready device.

"Nice job with the suitcase look," said Chaudry. "Even though it's not going on an airplane."

"Thanks. It does make it look harmless, doesn't it?" A thought struck him. "How *will* it be transported?"

"By boat to Naples. From there, by road to Paris."

"So it will be used in France? You told me Somalia."

Chaudry shrugged. "The plan has changed. But as I told you, it will never be detonated. It is for political leverage only."

It was awkward to be reminded that the device's lethal power was almost unlimited. Much better to think about how rich they were becoming.

It was lunchtime. Mirza's wife served them a light meal, masala dhosa and dhal, and then withdrew. They sat at Mirza's dining room table.

"How will you spend your money?" asked Chaudry, half joking.

Mirza was not amused. "I don't know. I haven't touched it yet."

Chaudry could tell that Mirza was uneasy about the whole thing. Too bad. The guy had taken the cash, after all.

He himself was made of tougher stuff, he thought. The way he looked at it, for centuries arms manufacturers had been making weapons to kill people. In Germany, Krupp had alternated between building armour-piercing shells and, a few years later, selling armour that could resist the shells. A few years after that, they would build a bigger shell, and so on.

He conveniently overlooked that this time was different because no armour could withstand a nuclear explosion.

44

———

November 2nd

Zidane was mulling over a list of targets in his mind.

It included the Arc de Triomphe, the Eiffel Tower and the Louvre, but also some less obvious sites. There was the Pompidou Centre, the Jeu de Paume Gallery, even the Folies Bergère music hall in Montmartre – the name itself would make a great headline.

He took out a street map and smoothed it on the kitchen table, anchoring it with mugs and a teapot. He wanted to figure out the area of destruction in each case and which streets would be affected.

It was at this point that he realised he did not really know the range of the device.

"When all else fails, read the instructions," his engineering professor had been fond of telling the class when he was a student.

The 'instructions' in this case consisted of a coded document that Mirza had sent to him and Chaudry by email. As a matter of prudence, it was important not to create paperwork that could be incriminating and Mirza had been warned to make the wording as bland and un-sinister as possible.

So Mirza had used some verbal camouflage. He described the device as a 'Domestic heating generator.' The text, which covered twelve pages including diagrams, did not use words like 'atomic' or 'nuclear.' But in the small print he found the information he needed:

'The unit has the capacity to service housing within a radius of half a mile, or six average city blocks.'

Paris, some of whose districts were many centuries old, was not a town that lent itself well to the idea of an average city block but Zidane understood well enough what was meant.

He considered the targets in turn, trying to assess each one's surroundings in terms of population density.

In one case his own flat was in the danger area, he noted with grim humour.

45

The following day, Zidane flew to Naples.

For the next phase of his project he needed a car. He looked in the yellow pages of the phone book. Ignoring the display ads of well known companies like Hertz and Avis, he telephoned a business that could apparently only afford a three line classified entry.

At a nondescript lot on the outskirts of Naples he picked out a white Fiat compact, one of the plainest cars on the lot. He chose it not to save money, but to be inconspicuous. He also selected a U-Haul style covered trailer big enough to contain the cargo of suitcases he was expecting.

He presented his papers to the clerk behind the desk. In his hotel room the night before, he had sorted through his aliases and set aside the papers relating to the identity of a Florida businessman of Cuban descent called Mario Perez. They were forgeries, but of high quality. He was confident that their serial numbers would not be run against a database for authenticity, as might have happened if he had gone to a bigger firm.

He drove to the port and approached the pier where several large freighters were moored. Parking the little car outside an office bearing the freshly painted placard *Miorini Freight Forwarding*, he went inside.

"Buon giorno." The receptionist looked barely twenty.

She was lusciously attractive with black hair and pale skin, her lips outlined in scarlet, framing perfect teeth. At another time, Zidane would have propositioned her but this was not the time or the place. Her beauty came as no surprise to him. He knew the tastes of the man he was about to meet.

Moments later Miorini himself appeared and ushered him into a private office.

The two men eyed each other across the table.

Miorini was in his late sixties, with wrinkled cheeks, thinning hair and watery blue eyes. There would have been very little character in his face except for the quizzical smile with which he regarded Zidane. It lit up his face and made him look sharply intelligent.

"How are you, Signor . . ." Miorini paused and looked at the card he had been handed. "Ah yes, Signor Perez." He spoke English with a slightly high pitched drawl. The faint smile again.

"Bene grazie. E lei?"

"Anch'io, molto bene."

Zidane nodded. He knew that Miorini knew his identity was false.

The Italian was one of a handful of people who were aware of his real identity.

Zidane had no friends. It was one reason he had survived for so long in the grey world of terrorism. But if he did have a friend, Miorini would have been that person, if only because they had known each other for forty years and, although both were professional assassins, neither had found it necessary to kill the other.

Miorini was an anarchist, an admirer of philosophers like Bakunin and Malatesta. As a young man and ardent trade unionist, he had practised his own brand of anarcho-syndicalism, fomenting strikes at Fiat and Olivetti with some success while managing to stay away from the limelight and out of prison. Once, he had hired the youthful Zidane to firebomb a Fiat warehouse and had been impressed by the Algerian's businesslike approach.

Now that he was older, Miorini had passed the baton to younger, more vigorous activists but at his core, the anarchist fires still smouldered.

Zidane knew this and when it became necessary to establish a freight forwarding firm in Naples for this project, he knew where to find his man. He used money from Fredy Mifuba to buy out the previous owner and so Miorini was now in charge.

Miorini said, "We unloaded your cargo, it's on a pallet in the warehouse."

"Good. Any problems?"

Miorini shook his head. "A minor weight disparity, but I'm guessing that's not an issue?"

"No," said Zidane shortly.

He watched as the suitcases were loaded into his trailer. A final wave to Miorini and he was on his way.

As Fiat and trailer pulled out of the yard, Miorini turned and walked back to his office looking thoughtful but not unhappy. There was obviously something extra in one of the suitcases but he had done nothing knowingly wrong. Although, he reflected, there must be a reason for the generous fifty thousand dollar fee that had been wired that morning to his Dubai account.

It was a fine sunny day with blue skies and a breath of spring in the air. Zidane was not given to flights of irrational exuberance but even so, he felt a surge of optimism as he guided the Fiat onto the Naples ring road leading towards the freeway and Switzerland.

46

Zidane switched on the car's GPS system.

Romanshorn was eleven hundred kilometres away – about seven hundred miles. Much of the route was along the Autostrada del Sole which connected Naples with Milan via Rome, Florence and Bologna. It was possible to get there in a day but that would be exhausting so he decided to stop overnight, probably close to Florence.

But first, he had a job to do. He stayed on surface roads for ten miles until he was out of town, then looked around for a wooded area.

Shortly he spotted a forest of poplars that, unlike most of the area, was not well kept. The undergrowth between the trees was thick and poorly maintained. It would serve his purpose.

He pulled off the road and turned down a rutted track that led deep into the trees. He stopped at an area of near-swamp, bordering on a pond fifty feet across. Its surface was covered in green slime and buzzing with mosquitoes.

Shielded from human gaze, he got out, unlocked the trailer and removed the most important suitcase, the one with the device. It was heavy, fifty pounds of dead weight, but he was able to manoeuvre it out of the trailer and into the Fiat's small trunk.

He re-closed the trailer and reversed both car and trailer closer to the pond until both were on the very edge, facing away from the water. Then he unfastened the trailer from the car.

Driving the Fiat carefully backwards, he nudged the trailer into the pond. It sank into the ooze and finally disappeared with a squelching sound. Swirls of algae re-formed across the pond's greasy surface and in a few minutes there was no disturbance to be seen.

He saw that he had left fresh tyre marks on the bank, so he drove onto drier ground and stopped. Breaking a branch off a nearby bush he raked it to and fro over the ground to obliterate the tell-tale tracks.

He was not able to remove all traces of his visit but very little remained to suggest that a large object – a trailer full of empty suitcases or anything else – had been dumped in the pond. The rental company would miss its trailer but it was no doubt insured and besides, the thing was far from new. One day perhaps the pond would dry out and the trailer would be found, but by then it would no longer matter.

· · ·

He resumed his journey. The Autostrada was the pride of the Italian road system. Very high speeds could be maintained and, given the Italians' love of fast cars, they often were. The little Fiat was capable of ninety miles an hour but Zidane had nothing to prove and was not given to bravado so he drove at a steady seventy-five, allowing faster cars to pass him at will.

Shortly before six pm he stopped outside Florence and checked into an American-style motel. He expected the food to be predictably bland but he was more concerned that the place had hot showers and CNN News that he could watch. He paid cash in advance, surprising the receptionist and causing her to ask for a two hundred euro security deposit. He paid, ungraciously but without complaining, in crisp fifty euro notes. The clerk found her guest's cold stare disturbing but company policy had to be observed.

After eating a passable steak, he lay on the bed in his room and watched as Wolf Blitzer described a terrorist incident in Turkey. A suicide bomber had walked up to a group of tourists and blown himself up near the Blue Mosque in Ankara, killing thirteen bystanders. Twelve of them had been German tourists. Zidane assumed that had been coincidence and not an anti-German plot but it was not really clear. He shook his head in disapproval. He personally felt that the many suicide incidents in recent years had disgusted the public rather than weakening their opposition and was thus futile.

His own exploits, although fewer in number, had

achieved just as much impact. They had also made him financially secure. In his twenties he had been an idealist but in time he had come to believe that few political causes were worth giving up his life for and certainly not those, like Al Qaeda and Daesh, whose leaders delegated suicide to their junior colleagues. Nowadays he thought of himself as a businessman and a survivor. Shaking his head at the wastefulness, he switched off the television and the light and enjoyed seven hours of untroubled sleep.

He set out at eight the next morning and made good time, stopping for five minutes every two hours to stretch his legs and maintain his concentration.

Around mid-morning he reached Como and entered Switzerland through the Italian speaking canton of Ticino.

Visually, there was not much change as he crossed the border. The street signs and advertisements continued to be in Italian for a while. Shortly, though, the scenery gave way to green hills punctuated by alpine chalets, white-steepled churches and well-groomed cows with bells around their necks. He was now in Graubünden, German-speaking and more mountainous. Here the appearance of the Swiss countryside had changed little in centuries – not surprising for a country which in 1999 had passed a referendum banning the building of mosques with minarets. That ban had attracted numerous challenges but fifteen years later it was still the law.

Shortly he entered Chur and stopped for lunch. He had promised himself a treat.

He made straight for the Hotel Stern on Reichsgasse and claimed a table at their restaurant the Büendner Stube. It was a homely place with fusty wood panelling and old fashioned décor but he knew its reputation for outstanding regional food. He had always been something of a gourmet, even as a student when he had come to ski in this area.

The treat was *Bündnerfleisch*, air-dried, paper-thin slices of raw red beef that would be hard to find anywhere outside the canton. Its preparation involved exposure to dry Alpine air for five weeks.

He could not resist exercising his language skills by ordering in Romansh, the fourth language of Switzerland after Swiss-German, French and Italian. Graubünden was the only canton where Romansh was one of the official languages. Barely one percent of Swiss people spoke it and the waiter, after his initial surprise, was clearly pleased. He made a point of attentively refilling Zidane's glass from his carafe of Pinot Gris from nearby Fläsch.

He had one more stop to make, but it was an important one. He had not confided to Munir Chaudry in Paris that he had another reason for choosing Romanshorn, namely that it was not far from the tiny principality of Liechtenstein. The road to Romanshorn ran through Vaduz, capital of the country whose population of 40,000 made it the fourth smallest in Europe after the Vatican, San Marino and Monaco. It had a sky high standard of living and more registered companies than citizens. He had business there.

He approached the offices of Schindler & Strauss, Attorneys, but stopped first for long enough to put away the papers relating to his Mario Perez identity. By the time he mounted the office steps, he was Doctor Otmar Schroeder, a Swiss physician living in Paris and a long-time client. He apologised for being a few minutes early but explained that he had an appointment with Werner Strauss, the senior partner.

Shown into the office of Herr Strauss, he switched languages again and greeted Strauss in the *Alemannic* dialect of German. This was the common language in Liechtenstein and differed both from standard German and the *Schweizerdeutsch* used in the German-speaking part of Switzerland.

Strauss nodded and shook hands. The Harvard-educated attorney could have conversed just as easily in English or several other languages but he smiled at the courtesy.

"How can I help you, Dr. Schroeder?"

"I want to make some changes to my portfolio."

Strauss nodded. He opened a file on his desk, adjusted his rimless glasses and studied it.

Zidane continued, "It is important that none of the investments appear in my name."

"That will be no problem. All your assets are held in the name of Crescent Holdings which is what in Liechtenstein we call an *Anstalt*, an entity of which you are the founder and sole owner." He smiled. "Crescent has only two directors and both of them are present in this room."

"I think I have cash and shares worth about six million dollars."

"Correct. The cash is actually in euros."

"Remind me, are any of the companies French?'

"Yes. I see Renault, Christian Dior and Michelin; also, two banks – BNP and Société Générale. Most of your holdings are worth substantially more than when you bought them."

"Sell them, just the French ones."

Strauss raised his eyebrows but nodded and jotted a note on his yellow legal pad.

"Very well. How should the proceeds be reinvested?"

"Convert the funds, along with my other cash, into American dollars."

"As you wish."

"Will there be any tax to pay?"

"No. Crescent is tax-exempt because it is an investment company with no economic activity in Liechtenstein."

"And must it report these transactions to any authority?"

Strauss shook his head again. "Crescent is not required to file accounts. It *is* supposed to have a statement of assets and liabilities available for inspection by the Liechtenstein Registrar of companies, but in practice, the Registrar does not exercise this right."

Zidane nodded. It was not total confidentiality, but he

realised the futility of disputing Liechtenstein law. Besides, he had the added protection of his fictional persona as Dr. Schroeder.

Strauss had not asked why he wanted to liquidate everything French. Zidane would not have expected him to. It was not how a Liechtenstein lawyer should behave.

They parted after some pleasantries and he continued his journey. He entered the canton of Thurgau at around four pm, passing briefly through its bustling capital, St. Gallen. Twenty minutes later he drove into the small town of Romanshorn.

Romanshorn, population 10,000, lay on the southern shore of Lake Constance, the long narrow lake that separated Switzerland from Germany. Its buildings were clean and its streets quiet.

Founded in the eighth century, originally agricultural but now relying on light industry and tourism, a quarter of its population were foreign nationals, the *Gastarbeiter* – guest workers – that Switzerland had relied on for years to man its industries.

He drove straight to the parcel store where he had for years rented a mailbox. Upon establishing his identity – he had become Mario Perez again – he was handed a parcel that had arrived for him from Pakistan labelled as horological machinery. Too large to fit into his mailbox, it had been waiting for him behind the counter, not in a secure enclosure, but so what? Theft was extremely rare in

Romanshorn and a simple package wrapped in brown paper was nothing for anyone to get excited about.

But Zidane *was* excited, he couldn't help it.

So far everything had gone as planned. Finally, he had both components of the device. Mated together, they would make a phenomenally destructive unit. All that remained was to carry them across the French-Swiss border to Paris where, properly configured, they would cause an explosion that would make all previous incidents look insignificant.

For the first time, he felt a twinge of anxiety. The consequences of getting caught with the hardware in his possession would be terminal. But there was no reason to panic, he just needed to keep his nerve. *I must be getting old*, he thought, *in the early days I would never even have contemplated failure.*

He was now only seven hours from Paris. He would bypass Zurich, cross the border at Basle, then drive past Besancon and straight into Paris on the A6. All signals were green.

He would be there tomorrow. Tonight he would allow himself a nice Swiss dinner.

47

When he arrived back in Paris, Zidane parked by the kerb outside his apartment.

Tired, he sat behind the wheel for a few minutes, just relaxing. It had been a long day. Dealing with stop-and-go city traffic had taken an hour in Paris alone.

He eyed his building's staircase. Getting the suitcase up four flights would be a project. Not the timing mechanism, he could carry that easily, but the suitcase would be a challenge. He knocked on the door of the concierge, Madame Dufour.

She was sitting in her poorly ventilated sitting room as she did every day, knitting or watching television, her pug dog, overweight like its mistress, snuffling around her ankles.

"Madame, this suitcase is quite heavy. It is full of belongings that I do not need in my flat. May I leave it in the storage room?"

She hoisted the spectacles that hung on a cord around her neck and perched them on her large nose. "I don't see why not, if there is nothing perishable inside, that is my only rule."

"Of course, Madame."

So that was taken care of. Only one issue remained – the rented car.

He did not need it any longer. His plan did call for a driver to take him to safety after he had planted the bomb, but for that, he would use Mansour, a low grade fellow who had his own vehicle, a Peugeot, and who knew nothing about the overall plan.

So he could abandon the Fiat, but not in Paris. It must not betray where it had taken its occupant. He sighed, that meant more driving and he was weary but there was nothing else for it. He set out again, this time armed with a flask of coffee and half a baguette containing camembert, his favourite. The destination: Rome.

The drive from Paris was thirteen hours, a long haul but it was necessary. He took a more southern route than before, via Lyon and Annecy, crossing the Italian border and stopping overnight near Genoa.

He made an early start next morning and got to Rome's Leonardo da Vinci airport around mid-day. He abandoned the car for the last time in the airport's long-term car park and bought a ticket to Paris, again paying cash for everything.

So after a two hour flight to Paris Orly, he was home in time for supper, tired but with a great sense of accomplishment. He now had in his possession a weapon of awesome strength obtained in total secrecy. He felt entitled to treat himself to dinner at Allard where he enjoyed roast duck with green olives and two glasses of champagne. He got home early, in good time to enjoy his usual sound night's sleep.

48

Ron Halfshaft looked at his watch. It was seven pm and he was at a loose end.

He had done enough programming for the day and now he was ready to relax. It was time for some gambling.

Oliver had mentioned Casino de France. Ron brewed some coffee, sat at the computer and googled *France* and *Casino*.

Casino de France was the first listing that came up. He grabbed a sheet of paper and wrote down the address, Rue des Abbesses in the Pigalle area. He was so gripped by the prospect of playing some blackjack that he did not fully read the Wikipedia entry. That was a mistake.

His taxi stopped outside a colonnaded facade and he

stepped into what looked like a theatre foyer with a ticket window in one corner.

He approached a uniformed commissionaire and spoke in his precise but atrociously accented French, "Which way are the tables?"

"M'sieu?"

"The tables. You know, blackjack, craps."

The man looked mystified for a minute, then his face cleared.

"Ah, but I regret, this is not that kind of casino."

"This is the Casino de France, right?"

'Yes sir, but we are not for gambling. This is what you would call in English a 'music hall.'

"Music hall? It says you are a casino." He pointed to the neon sign above the entrance.

The commissionaire smiled. "I understand the confusion but this is one of the oldest theatres of its kind and is known all over France. Casino de France has been our name for many years. A thousand apologies."

Halfshaft was disappointed. He had been looking forward to playing cards and finding out how his unique skills would work in a European setting.

But he was also intrigued. Besides, it was getting late and he had nowhere else to go.

"Well, okay. What's your show tonight?"

The man pointed to a poster. "The ballet, 'Swan Lake Reloaded', starts in fifteen minutes. Your timing is perfect."

"Swan Lake? Well it's not what I was expecting."

"This is a modern production by a Swedish director, with the swans played as prostitutes."

Halfshaft shrugged. He was up for anything so he bought a ticket and a program and moments later was sitting in the red plush auditorium, waiting for the show to start.

From the program, he learned that the first theatre on this site had been built in the 18th Century. Over the years, it had featured such performers as Mistinguett, Josephine Baker and Maurice Chevalier.

The curtain rose to the music of Tchaikovsky. He found himself enjoying the show despite, or perhaps because of, the liberties taken with the original including Odette's struggle with heroin addiction and the brazen dancing of the chorus of hookers.

At the interval, he went to the bar and ordered a pastis. He leaned on the counter and sipped the aniseed drink feeling quite French.

He became aware of a man, slight and unprepossessing, who stood to his left by the bar drinking coffee. The fellow was glancing around the room in an oddly analytical way, as if mentally taking measurements.

Halfshaft had never been backward in coming forward and liked to chat with anyone, so he grinned agreeably, making eye contact in a way that made it hard for the guy to ignore him. "Good show, huh?"

The man nodded. He did not seem to want to talk.

"They sure took some liberties with Tchaikovsky, though."

"Quite so." The man's accent was not French but Half-shaft guessed that English was not his mother tongue either.

"Where are you from?" asked Halfshaft.

No reply.

"Guess you're a ballet fan, seeing as you're here?"

A half smile in response.

"Me, I'm here by mistake. I thought this was a gambling casino, can you believe? Teach me to do some research before running out of the house!"

"Research? Ah my friend, that is essential to any project."

The words were spoken with feeling and Halfshaft felt he had struck a nerve, but the man fell silent again as if wishing he had not spoken. Halfshaft tried again, "You're not from here are you? I'm from the U.S.A."

"Which state?" asked the man automatically.

"California. And you?"

"All over," the man smiled.

At that point the bell rang for the second act and the two men returned to their seats, which were in different rows some way apart.

The second act was as lively as the first and, at the end, the cast took several curtain calls. Halfshaft applauded enthusiastically before shuffling towards the exit with the rest of the audience.

On the way out he spotted his companion from the

interval. The man was queuing at the cloakroom. Halfshaft saw him retrieve a large suitcase. He thought that a little strange but he could not put his finger on a reason and he put it out of his mind.

He lingered awhile outside, reading the posters for future performances. Most referred to singers he did not recognise, although the name Sheryl Crow stood out since he enjoyed her country music songs.

Another name that rang a bell was Christiane Rouget. He had an idea she was a celebrity, and made a note to ask Oliver who was into current affairs and was sure to know.

As he was reading, the man with the suitcase emerged and walked past him.

"Have a great rest of the evening," said Halfshaft.

The man acknowledged him with a nod, not rude but not friendly either. Odd people, the French. Or wherever the guy was from? That's right, he never did say.

The man was handling the large suitcase with ease. He was slim and not tall so he must be stronger than he looked.

Either that or the suitcase was empty.

49

When all else fails, do something. I had an idea and called Tisch.

"What's up?" He sounded irritated.

"I want to run a plan by you."

"It's nine o'clock at night."

"It's urgent."

"You had better come round."

I don't know if General Choltitz occupied the Presidential Suite when the Meurice was the German Army headquarters but it seems possible. The decor is in the style of Louis XVI. Crystal chandeliers hang from the ceiling. Silk in oyster and silver hues is everywhere. The furniture would grace a palace. Full-length windows overlook the Tuileries Garden.

When I arrived, the moon had risen and the trees were bathed in moonlight. Tisch opened the door and beckoned me in. He held an open can of Red Stripe. His tee shirt looked as if it was on its third or fourth day.

I sniffed. "They probably have a laundry here."

He scowled. "What's up?"

"We have to find Zidane."

"Or?"

"Or we'll all be vaporised."

Mimi was listening. "Shouldn't we go to the police?"

"Welcome to getting trampled in the mad dash for the airport!" said Tisch.

Mimi looked shocked. "Surely people are more civilised than that?"

"Don't count on it," I said.

"Let's review," said Carlton. "No use looking under Z in the phone book. What leads do we have? What about Chaudry?"

"Chaudry only knows what he has already told us."

"That leaves the people building this dreadful thing."

"Whose address I have." I waved the paper Chaudry had given me.

"What are you saying?" said Tisch.

"Maybe I should pay these guys a call."

"In person?"

"Do you have a better idea?"

"It's a long way."

"I'm up for it."

I had never been to Pakistan. I had been to India – Delhi for the Commonwealth Games, and some tiger watching in Kerala – but that was it.

"Fly economy, it's only six hours." Tisch can be a real cheapskate when it comes to other people.

I shook my head. "Business class."

I pointedly eyed the scalloped silk curtains and Persian carpets. The bathroom was solid marble.

"Done. Time is short, get the next flight."

I had the hotel make a reservation for me in Islamabad. The assistant manager, a seriously attractive young Frenchwoman in thick glasses called my attention to an official U.S. travel advisory which said: "The Department of State warns U.S. citizens to defer all non-essential travel to Pakistan."

An encouraging start! Still, my trip *was* essential. Besides, I had a British as well as an American passport. This time, I would use the British one.

I had intended to stay at the Marriott at the airport because it sounded convenient but the manager frowned prettily. "You should try the Serena Hotel."

"Have you stayed there?" I knew that hotel employees often got preferential rates in other hotels and were able to do a good deal of high class travelling.

She nodded. "It's very elegant. Top of the line, with excellent food but no alcohol in the public areas which is normal in Pakistan, being a Moslem country. And the security is first class."

"Why so much emphasis on security?" I asked.

She smiled. "You will see when you get there."

At eight next morning I headed off to Charles de Gaulle, bound for Islamabad.

On the plane I read up on Pakistan.

In 1947, India split into two countries along religious lines, India and Pakistan. There has been hostility between them ever since.

They are both among the nine countries known or believed to have nuclear weapons.

In 1974, Pakistan grew very nervous when India conducted a nuclear test, codename 'Smiling Buddha.' They responded by hiring a German-trained engineer, A. Q. Khan, to develop a supply of enriched uranium for nuclear weapons. Khan brought plans for centrifuges back to Pakistan and started an enrichment programme. The Khan Research Laboratory, KRL, is still Pakistan's main weapons research facility, managed by the Army. It is based in Kahuta, near Islamabad.

The Prime Minster, Zulfikar Ali Bhutto was later deposed and executed. His daughter Benazir Bhutto became Prime Minster too, but was assassinated in a bombing. Which illustrates that Pakistani politics are messy. The same is true of its attitude towards nuclear matters.

A. Q. Khan became Science Advisor to the Government but was fired in 2004 following reports that Pakistan had sold nuclear secrets to other countries. He confessed on television to having transferred technology to Iran,

Libya and North Korea. But a short while later President Musharraf awarded him a presidential pardon, conveying an oddly mixed message.

I found all this on the Internet. It alerted me that I could be walking into a tricky situation.

Carlton's estimate of a six hour journey was ridiculous. The flight to Qatar alone was six hours. Then a two hour stopover in Qatar and finally three hours from Qatar to Islamabad, eleven hours in all. Qatar's smart new airport is very nice but because of the time difference it was two the next morning when I got to Islamabad.

The manageress in Paris was right about security. The minute I stepped off the plane it was apparent. No one except those travelling were allowed in the airport's arrival area. I waited in line at a supervised official taxi stand, then watched as first the interior and then the boot of my vehicle were inspected. A metal scanner on a long pole was thrust under the bottom of the car to search for possible explosives. Finally, it was declared safe and I boarded for the twelve mile journey to my hotel.

The outside of the Serena certainly looked impressive but I was in no mood to appreciate it. The world could be coming to an end but I was *really* tired. I was barely able to notice that my room was the last word in luxury before I fell into bed and slept for seven hours prior to surfacing the next day.

50

In the morning there was more security.

There was no taxi stand outside the hotel entrance. Access was designed so that there was only one way in and one way out, both tightly controlled. When I asked for a taxi I was told politely but firmly that the hotel would provide one of its official registered cars. I asked why this was.

The bell captain smiled. "Kidnapping in Pakistan is a lucrative business, especially with foreigners. We will give the driver the address and you will reach your destination safely."

"He will have to wait for me when we get there, possibly for several hours, and bring me back."

"No problem."

I watched again as the interior and boot of my car were inspected and the scanner passed underneath for possible explosives.

Finally, we got under way. My driver was a tall Afghan type in his thirties, and seemed good natured. He wore the traditional shalwar kameez – loose fitting trousers and calf-length tunic – with a waistcoat over the tunic. It was a cool morning and he also had a brown woolen shawl wrapped around his shoulders.

Before we drew away from the curb I leaned forward and showed him my sheet of paper with the address. It was actually a photocopy of the original scrap of paper from Chaudry, enlarged for just this purpose. He smiled and said nothing.

"It's in Urdu, see?" I handed him my map as backup.

I could have saved myself the trouble. He stared at it upside down. I turned it right way up for him. He frowned politely. I wondered if he was illiterate.

We set off. My fingers were crossed, but we covered the thirty miles to Kahuta without incident and arrived at a small house in a residential street. There were no street names or numbers to be seen but the driver seemed confident, much more so than me.

"Wait here," I said.

I knocked on the door.

It opened and a young woman smiled enquiringly.

She looked several months pregnant. She apparently assumed that I was Anglo Saxon because she spoke in English.

"Yes?"

"Is this the home of Rashid Mirza?"

"Yes of course. You must be from the laboratory."

"Not exactly, but I do need to see Rashid."

She nodded. "Come in. I expect you want to talk. Anyway, I am packing for our trip. Will you have some tea, or a soft drink?"

What trip?

"Tea would be nice."

A man appeared behind her. This must be who I had come to see. I was briefly tongue-tied. I produced a card, feeling foolish. "My name is Oliver Steele."

"Yes, what can I do for you?"

This was not like meeting Munir Chaudry. Mirza seemed direct, confident, mildly curious about an unexpected visitor.

"Can we talk? It's a technical matter." I glanced at the woman.

She nodded. "I'll make tea."

"Come into the office."

He turned and led the way. The house was small. His den contained a desk, a drawing board and some metal filing cabinets. I noticed that they all had locks. A computer with a flat screen monitor stood on the desk. A sheet of clean white paper was on the drawing board. Next to it, open, was a leather case containing drawing instruments – compass, dividers, a protractor.

He saw me looking at them and laughed. "I still use the old manual ways sometimes. It helps me relax. Even though everything is CAD now."

"CAD?"

"Computer Assisted Design. I take it you are not an engineer?"

I shook my head.

"So what's up, my friend?"

"I need to confirm something."

His eye fixed on me.

I nodded. "I have reason to believe that you built, or helped to build, a nuclear device and sold it to a terrorist."

The temperature in the warm room – there was no air conditioning – fell about twenty degrees.

He smiled thinly and shook his head. "I don't know where you heard that, but it is nonsense."

I took a sheet of paper from my pocket and continued.

"You received two large payments of four hundred thousand dollars each."

"As I said, nonsense." But his eye no longer met mine.

"The first payment was made about a month ago and the second last week."

I was sure of my facts, having obtained chapter and verse from Chaudry in Paris, so I spoke with confidence. That must have been clear to Mirza because his attitude changed. His face showed a mixture of emotions: surprise, anger, some fear. He toyed silently with an empty coffee mug. When he spoke it was to show defiance.

"If you know all that, then you probably know that Pakistan has been selling nuclear technology to foreign countries for years."

"Does that make it right?"

He shrugged. "I had an opportunity and I took it."

"The fact that you received a second payment suggests that you have delivered the product."

"Yes, what of it?"

"Aren't you concerned about the loss of life?"

He shrugged. "That won't happen."

"How can you be sure?"

"It is only for use as a deterrent. Keep in mind that, even with thousands of nuclear bombs in the world, since 1945 none have ever been used in anger."

"This time may be different," I said.

He shook his head. "The device I built is strictly for intimidation. It will never be used."

"Who told you that? Munir Chaudry?"

He nodded, clearly recognising the name.

"Who exactly are you?" he asked.

I ignored the question. "You can tell from my presence that many things you thought were confidential are nothing of the kind. We know exactly what you did and how much you were paid."

There was a knock at the door. Mirza's wife entered with a tray of tea things. She was attractive and pleasant without being aggressive and I warmed to her.

"Did Rashid tell you about our trip?" she asked.

I shook my head.

"Yes, we're going around the world. He has worked so hard, never taking a holiday, and his year-end bonus was very generous, so I persuaded him. It will be our last chance before the baby arrives."

I know all about that bonus, I thought. I glanced at Mirza who fidgeted.

When she was gone, I said, "Look, I can see that you've been misled. I don't think you are a bad person, so I am going to explain the facts and together we shall see what can be done."

Privately I was not sure about the 'not a bad person' bit. He had been reckless and greedy at best. Just when that amounted to 'bad' was a nice question.

"The bomb's destination is Paris, and it will be detonated there if we don't prevent it." I spoke quietly, but his face went white.

"How and when was it sent?" I asked.

"Five days ago, by ship from Karachi. I drove it there in my truck and supervised the loading myself."

"Do you have the shipping documents?"

He unlocked one of the file drawers and took out a manila folder. "Here."

He teased out a smudgy printed form and handed it to me. It was a bill of lading in English and Urdu. I scanned it. The cargo was described as 'Suitcases, quantity 24.'

"Suitcases?"

Mirza explained the deception, which involved hiding the device in a shipment of suitcases in order to be as inconspicuous as possible.

"The boat must have reached Naples by now," I said.

He checked the date on his digital watch. "Actually, not yet. It is quite a long journey via the Red Sea and the Suez Canal. But it should arrive in the next twenty-four hours."

I got up. "In that case, there is no time to lose. My guess is that the purchaser will personally take delivery at Naples and transport it to Paris."

"Then you can intercept him, with it in his possession."

"Possibly." I was not going to tell Mirza that I had no idea where Zidane was, but clearly, my best chance would be to confront him in Italy. After that, there was no knowing where he might be. I had to get to Naples quickly. Pocketing the bill of lading, I headed for the door.

Mirza followed me. "What shall I do?"

"Nothing. You've done quite enough."

"What will happen to me?"

"In any other country you would be tried and convicted of selling military data to foreign parties. But in Pakistan? It's hard to say."

I brushed past him, beckoned my driver and climbed into the car for the journey back to Islamabad.

As Mirza stood in the doorway, the last words I heard were, "Will I be able to keep the money?"

51

My journey to Naples was a scheduling nightmare.

The first leg, a flight to Abu Dhabi, left Islamabad at 3:40 in the morning. I endured a staggeringly dull three hour layover before proceeding to Rome where I hitched a ride on an Alitalia Airbus. Altogether the trip took seventeen hours.

I tried to get some sleep on the journey, knowing there would be no time when I landed. I snatched an hour here and there but it was shallow and disjointed, providing little rest.

At Naples I rented a Fiat and drove to the office of Miorini Freight Forwarding.

I flourished my bill of lading. The painted young brunette at the desk did not seem very interested.

"That shipment has been cleared already."

"By whom?"

She frowned. "Who wants to know?"

I bit my tongue. "Where is the manager?"

A man appeared, so quickly that he must have been listening. He was in his sixties, thin and sharp-eyed.

He was the not the first wrongdoer I had confronted in my quest but somehow he struck me as the most disturbing. The others had been amateurs, sucked by greed into an epic misstep but I sensed that this man knew exactly what he was doing and did not care. At least part sociopath. Before I met him I had wondered if he was a close colleague of Zidane and now that I saw him I was sure of it.

Well, it was all or nothing. "In your office?" I asked.

He nodded.

I got in his face, standing very close. "You know what was in those suitcases, don't you!"

"No idea," he smiled.

He moved towards his desk. I moved sideways with him. He reached down and made to open a drawer. I grabbed his arm and twisted it, shoving him away.

He muttered something in Italian.

By now I was angry, besides being tired and out of sorts. I pulled open the drawer. Inside was a small but deadly Glock G29 pistol with silencer attached. I grabbed it before he could and rounded on him.

"Where is Zidane?"

He shook his head.

I shot him in the left shoulder.

From the way he staggered I could tell that the bullet

had lodged in bone rather than passing straight through. His face went dead white.

"I don't think anyone heard," I said. "The next one is for the other shoulder."

"He was here but he left. I don't know where." His voice was faint.

"How was he travelling?"

"He had a car and trailer."

"What kind of trailer? How large? What brand?"

"It was a Kwik-Haul. A two wheeler that you tow behind your car. "

"So what happened?"

"What do you think? He loaded the suitcases."

"And one of them was unusually heavy, right?"

He nodded, his face sagging. I would not get much more out of him.

I guessed that Zidane would ditch the unwanted suitcases immediately and drive back to Paris by the quickest route.

I left Miorini's office, shutting the door. Outside I told the woman, "He needs you, better go in."

She gave me a look and hurried inside.

I got into my car and drove off quickly. Discretion was important, I didn't want them identifying my vehicle. They did not seem like the kind of people who would call the authorities but I couldn't be sure and the last thing I needed was to be arrested by the Italian police for shooting someone, no matter how sleazy.

I racked my brains as I drove. I had to think of a way to get onto Zidane's trail but so far I had nothing.

I tried to put myself in his shoes. Suppose it was me, not Zidane, coming from Paris. I would fly to Naples, but I would probably research cars and trailers before I set out, to avoid the risk of not being able to find one. Not every rental company had trailers, in fact, it was exceptional.

I used my mobile phone to call Kathy.

"Hi! Do me a favour, run a Google search for Kwik-Haul renting firms near Naples airport."

"Sure. What's the story?"

"If I can find out where he rented his trailer, I may get a line on what his car looks like."

She called me back ten minutes later. "You may be onto something. There's only one agency near the airport for that brand of trailer. Here's the number."

"You're a star!"

I called Kwik-Haul.

"I am afraid there has been an accident. It involves one of your trailers."

"One moment, I will pass you to my manager."

A man's voice, "Pronto?"

I took a deep breath and prepared to lie for France. "Oh, thank goodness. I am calling from the scene of a bad accident. A car hauling one of your trailers went off the road into a tree and caught fire. The driver managed to escape from the car but he is badly burned. I don't know if he will survive."

"That is dreadful. How can I help?"

"We are trying to identify the driver. The fire was intense and unfortunately all the paperwork has been burned, but we can still read the Kwik-Haul symbol on the trailer. Since we are near the airport, we are calling your office to see if you can help us. Did you, by any chance, rent such a trailer recently?"

"I understand. Respectfully, what is your place in all this?"

I had expected the question. "I was the first person to pass by. I have telephoned the ambulance and they are coming. I am calling you because we need to identify the driver and notify his relatives. Hopefully, they will be able to get to the hospital in time."

I was developing quite a taste for this fictionalising, almost sobbing with emotion as I spoke. Dial it down, I told myself, don't overdo things.

I seemed to have captured the manager's sympathy because he said, "Let me check."

He came back. "Well, you're in luck, if I can use that expression. A man rented one of our trailers earlier today."

"What can you tell me about him?"

"His name was Mario Perez, an American. He rented a white Fiat compact and a Kwik-Haul. He wanted to pay cash but we insisted on a credit card, it is how we do business."

"Do you have the car's registration? Although the car is badly burned, the police may be able to use that to make a positive ID."

"It is ADFR22. An Italian number, of course."

Finally, in as offhand a tone as I could muster, I asked.
"What's his address?"

"It is in Paris, Rue du Parc-de-Montien."

I held my breath. "What is the street number?"

There was silence. Then, "That is all I can tell you. We have security constraints. I think I have given you enough information for your needs."

So that was all I was going to get. I was dealing with a cautious bureaucrat. I could hear the note of self-satisfaction in his voice as he politely slapped me down. It was time for a gracious withdrawal.

"Thank you so much. You have been enormously helpful sir. I am sure the police will be calling you."

"No problem. I only just started my shift, so I shall be here. I shall need their information anyway for my report. There are insurance issues, you understand."

"Of course."

I rang off and called Kathy.

"We're in business – sort of. Here's the number of a white Fiat compact that should be arriving at Rue du Parc-de-Montien some time shortly, driven by Zidane."

"What use is that? It's a very long street."

"I understand. You will have to enlist Goldhawk and get help. At least we know that we're looking for a Fiat, license ADFR22. Put watchers on every corner around the clock. It's our best hope."

She understood immediately. "I'm on it. What about you, are you coming back?"

"On the next flight."

. . .

I arrived at Charles de Gaulle later that evening and took a cab straight to the Meurice.

It was a strange feeling coming back to a city, one of the most civilised in the world as well as the most beautiful, knowing that it was in danger of destruction. The evening was warm and crowds strolled to and fro on the boulevards or sat at cafes and restaurants, animated and oblivious to the looming disaster.

I couldn't help thinking of von Choltitz, the ambivalent German general who, as military governor, was ordered by Hitler to burn Paris to the ground rather than surrender it to the Free French.

He had defied Hitler's order.

He was asked after the war why he had disobeyed Hitler. He said that he loved Paris and also he was convinced by then that Hitler was insane. On the whole, history and the Allies dealt leniently with him. He spent time in prison but was released in 1947 with no specific charges ever being filed. When he died in 1966, several high ranking French officers attended his funeral.

Was Zidane insane? You or I might think so. But there could be thousands of Palestinians who resented Israel's existence, or perhaps the way in which Israeli settlements had been built on land beyond the original boundaries of Israel. They might have a more nuanced opinion about extremists like Zidane. Not for nothing had the Israeli-Palestinian situation been described as the most intractable dispute in history. So was Zidane fanatical? Deluded? Certainly in the grip of an overriding passion. Whatever the case, his cunning was beyond question and at this stage in his life he was probably more dangerous than ever.

In Tisch's suite I wanted to convey a sense of urgency but I need not have worried. He had grasped the point.

"We've got people on the block already," he said crisply.

"How many?"

"Ten. In plain clothes, strolling around, keeping their eyes skinned for a white Fiat, plate number ADFR22."

Kathy asked, "When do you think he will arrive?"

"Hard to say. If he drives nonstop from Naples he could be in Paris by dawn tomorrow but we should allow for stops or even a detour. We just don't know his plans."

"The watchers are on eight hour shifts," said Tisch. "They will be replaced periodically. We'll keep things covered until he shows up even if it takes a week."

I went to the window and looked out at the Tuileries Garden.

"We've been doing all this on our own until now," I said. "Do you think it's time we told the authorities?"

Tisch wrinkled his nose. "It means losing control."

"But we need the manpower. It will take dozens of people to keep up the level of surveillance that we need."

"I'm not saying you're wrong," said Tisch. "Leave it to me, I'll work out a way."

"It would help if we could narrow the search area," said Kathy. " Rue du Parc-de-Montien spans ten blocks and is a mile and a half long. If we knew within a couple of blocks where his apartment was, things would be much easier."

I suddenly realised I hadn't slept in a while. "I'm going back to my hotel. You can reach me there if you must, but otherwise I shall be dead to the world until tomorrow."

The phone rang by my bed. The red digital clock on the nightstand said six am.

"It's Tisch."

"Thanks for letting me sleep in," I said.

"I spoke to Goldhawk."

"Did you wake him up too?"

"No, we rich guys work a full day, not like some."

I rubbed sleep from my eyes. "What do you want?"

"He knows the Prefect of Police for Paris."

"Bully for him."

"It's the right level at which to engage law enforcement. It's arranged; we're meeting him at the Préfecture at eight am. Be there. Try and dig up a clean shirt."

The Préfecture was an imposing mansard-roofed building of grey stone facing onto Place Louis Lépine on the Île de la Cité. I had to identify myself to a pair of blue-uniformed guards at a pillbox on the sidewalk. When I said I had an appointment with the Préfet, or Prefect, eyebrows were raised but I had brought my passport expecting something like that. After a phone call to someone inside and checking my resemblance to my five year old photo, not a great likeness, they waved me through.

I found the others inside. We waited for a while in a high-ceilinged anteroom, staring at the white and gold mouldings. I wore a jacket and tie and so to my slight surprise did Tisch. Goldhawk was in jeans and a dress shirt but no tie, maybe he was well in with the Prefect and it didn't matter, I don't know.

After five minutes we were ushered into the presence.

Jean Villeneuve, the top policeman in Paris, was slim and dapper, fifty, clean shaven with pink cheeks and a cap of black hair slicked back. Introductions were made. He had a face like a bank clerk but that impression was dispelled as soon as he spoke, in faultless English.

"Jimmy and I are used to getting up early, we shoot duck together sometimes which entails a pre-dawn rendezvous. But I understand this is more serious."

Goldhawk said, "You are aware that I have good sources of information. It's necessary for my business."

Villeneuve nodded.

"I've just learned of some financial transactions involving the terrorist Zidane."

Villeneuve frowned. "It's a while since I heard that name. To tell you the truth, I hoped he was dead."

"I understand. Unfortunately, he seems to be active, in fact, he poses an immediate threat."

"Ah." Villeneuve waited.

Goldhawk nodded. "I confided in my old friend from

America, Mr. Tisch, who is visiting Paris. With the help of his advisor Oliver Steele" – he nodded at me – "we've put together a picture of Zidane's recent actions and his plans, which are very troubling. I'll let Mr. Steele bring us up to date."

I described my meeting with cultural attaché Chaudry, my trip to Pakistan and my confrontation with the young nuclear engineer. Finally, I explained that Zidane was either in, or on his way to Paris with a weapon of mass destruction.

I ended by stressing the key fact. "Within the next twenty-four hours this man and his weaponry will be here. If we don't intercept him, thousands may die."

Villeneuve did not waste time chiding us for not contacting him sooner and I credited him for that.

"Two things," he said. "First, we must find him. We shall bring everything possible to bear in the way of manpower and resources. Second, for the sake of civil order, as few people as possible must know about this."

"I'm glad you understand," I said. "I was afraid that you would flood the streets with gendarmes. Zidane is sophisticated and has sharp instincts, so anything of that kind would certainly be detected. He would just melt quietly away, more dangerous than ever and even harder to find."

Villeneuve smiled politely. He did not say that my comment was obvious, but I felt a bit foolish having said it. He presided over a city that had endured more than its share of terrorism. He didn't need a lecture from me.

"Do you have enough lookouts on Montien?" he asked.

"We could use another shift," said Goldhawk. "But we must take care not to alert our quarry."

"What have you told your watchers as to why they are there?"

Goldhawk said, "They think they are looking for an individual who has embezzled money from one of my companies."

Villeneuve nodded. "Whatever works." He stood up. "I shall have to inform the Minister of Justice. Please continue with your surveillance. I shall need hourly reports."

Goldhawk and Tisch both looked at me and I nodded.

I didn't much relish being a messenger boy, but at least I could bill Tisch for my time.

52

K athy was getting impatient.

She was more and more frustrated at the lack of progress in finding Zidane and she recognised the price of failure with gut-wrenching clarity.

She decided to do something rather than nothing. She would head for Rue du Parc-de-Montien where Gold-hawk's security men were now patrolling, in hope of finding the terrorist herself.

She put herself in Zidane's place, trying to think like him. It was a technique she sometimes used, pretending she really *was* the person. It was more than just standing in his shoes - she tried to get inside his head.

What was he feeling? What basic idea inspired him? She knew that Oliver and Tisch had both tried in their own ways to ask the same thing. But while she respected their business skills, she questioned their powers of insight.

Zidane was getting older. The days of his reputation as a young firebrand were long gone. People evolve, why should terrorists be any different?

Did he mean this to be his last hurrah, she wondered? What if the years had convinced him that there was no permanent victory, the forces of capitalism were just too strong? If he thought that, perhaps he intended to go out, finally, in a blaze of glory?

How highly did he value his own life?

Maybe not so much. What were the implications of that? What if he didn't plan to leave Paris before the explosion. What if he was willing to go up in smoke along with his victims?

She took the Metro, getting down at Porte d'Orleans, and walked the few yards to the eastern end of Montien.

It was a long street and her heart sank as she watched it stretch into the distance. Where on earth to start?

She pulled out her phone and called Ron Halfshaft.

"Yo?" He sounded rushed, as usual.

"Got a challenge for you."

"I never fail."

"Wait 'til you hear it."

"Shoot."

"I'm standing on a street that is over a mile long, trying to find the address of a man whose name I don't know."

"How tall are the buildings?"

"Gee, about fifty feet. Who cares?"

He sounded impatient. "How many floors?"

She looked harder, examining the grey houses for the first time. They were terraced rather than free-standing.

"Four. Five if you include the garrets."

"Does your man own or is he renting?"

"Probably renting."

"House or apartment?"

"Apartment."

"Does he have a family?"

"I doubt it. More of a loner."

"Does he own a car?"

"Probably not."

"Does he like to cook?"

"No idea. I don't know the guy that well," she protested.

"But he's a loner, right?"

"For sure."

"In that case, look for buildings with small apartments, within walking distance of a metro station, close to a grocery store and some moderately priced restaurants."

He's making sense, she thought. "That'll narrow it down. Thanks."

"No problem. I'll check with Goldhawk's computer guys to see if there's a database that might help."

"Good! Maybe there's something public that you could, like, scan."

"Public, private, whatever. Not much I can't take a peek at."

"Even in France, a foreign country?"

He chortled. "Numbers are numbers, baby."

She shook her head. She wished he didn't sound quite so cocky. "Call me if you find anything."

"Roger that."

She was already standing near the Metro station, so she met Halfshaft's first condition. Which way should she start walking – east or west? There were restaurants in both directions. She took out a one euro coin and flipped it, telling herself, 'heads east, tails west.'

It came to rest on the sidewalk showing a picture of a naked man with his legs apart. She recognised da Vinci's famous image illustrating the proportions of the human body. An Italian euro.

Was that heads or tails? The other side bore a figure 1 and a map of Europe. No help. But the little man, besides being anatomically correct, had a head, and heads meant east. She started walking.

She covered fifty yards without incident. Where were Goldhawk's people? They would be inconspicuous of course. She passed a woman pushing a pram and, coming the other way, a young man with a satchel, maybe full of books. A student. Or not. Detectives in the movies had earpieces with little curly cords. The woman and the young man both had shoulder length hair so that didn't help.

Lost in thought, she almost walked past a white Fiat

compact parked by the kerb. Then she remembered that she was looking for registration number ADFR22, so she bent down to read the plate. But it was a different number, not the plate she was looking for. She stood up slowly.

As she did so, she felt a hand on her arm.

53

November 11th

We were in Carlton's suite – Carlton, Mimi, Ron and I – trying to figure out not just when Zidane would make his move, but also, where the heck was Kathy?

On top of everything else, she seemed to have disappeared.

"Let's keep calm," I said. But I wasn't feeling too calm.

We had been trying to raise her by phone all day without success. Some people don't return calls but she was not like that, quite the opposite in fact, so it was worrying.

The mood was sombre. We all knew that the clock was

ticking. Now that Zidane had the bomb there was no reason why he would not use it.

Tisch said, "He has the device. And it's possible, since we haven't heard from her, that Kathy has become his captive."

"We don't know that for certain," said Mimi.

"It's probable," he said shortly.

I said. "It's unlike her not to get in touch. She's a talkative girl and a ready communicator. She would have called in if she were able."

"Do you think she's alive?" asked Mimi.

There was an awkward silence. Tisch and I looked at each other.

"We just don't know," I said.

More silence.

Mimi said, "There's one reason Zidane may not act right away."

"What's that," barked Carlton. He could be short with his wife.

But she could handle him.

Carlton had a habit in the heat of debate of talking at people rather than to them. But he had learned not to do that with Mimi. Possibly because she had once reminded him sweetly that she could always go back to her strong nuclear family of parents and siblings in Huddersfield. One warning had been enough. Carlton had no similar support group, being the only child of parents long deceased and he was secretly envious of anyone who had.

Quietly she said, "He's got to communicate with

Chaudry, tell him when to leave town. Chaudry is still in Paris. If we see him getting ready to run for it, we'll know something's about to happen."

"Exactly," said Halfshaft, whose mind was binary. He liked logic, it solved all problems.

I was less sure. "A promise from Zidane isn't worth a pitcher of warm spit, as they say in Texas."

Mimi frowned. "Meaning?"

"Meaning that he owes no loyalty to anyone, and certainly not to Chaudry. The diplomat has served his purpose. For all Zidane cares, Chaudry can disappear in a puff of smoke."

"Literally," said Carlton.

More silence.

I said, "Let's ask ourselves how we would use the device if we were Zidane."

"I hate to go there," said Mimi.

"Do you have a better idea?"

"How would he get the most bang for the buck, pardon the expression?" mused Halfshaft.

"He'd blow up a monument," said Carlton quietly. "Remember Hitler's plans for Paris? When he ordered Choltitz to burn it down, he was really telling him to concentrate on prominent buildings. The Eiffel Tower was rigged with explosives."

"How does that help us?" asked Mimi. "We can't go and stand in front of Sacré-Coeur, the Arc de Triomphe and every other prominent building and wait for him to stroll up with his suitcase. We don't have the manpower."

"We would if we used the police. Villeneuve could set it up."

I said. "And how will Zidane react if he sees uniformed police blocking him and his suitcase?

"He'd run like hell," said Mimi.

"Exactly. He'd go somewhere else. We have to assume he has a Plan B. I would, in his shoes," I said.

We were looking for a needle in the haystack that was Paris and the odds against us were long. But sitting and waiting was not an option. We had to try.

Mimi looked at her watch. "It's mid-day and it's Friday. Driving through the city will shortly get really slow. If we're going to involve the police, we had better act quickly."

Tisch picked up the hotel's white telephone. "Get me Villeneuve at the Préfecture. I called him yesterday, you must have the number."

Within the hour, plainclothes police fanned out, to stand and overlook the entrances to many of Paris's most recognisable buildings – the Eiffel Tower, the Jeu de Paume, the Quai d'Orsay, the Louvre, the Pompidou Centre, Sacré-Coeur, both Opera houses – the original on Place de l'Opéra and the newer one near the Bastille – and others. But it was with faint hope that I listened to Tisch and the Prefect arranging things. We knew how easily the fish could slip through the net.

Back at the Meurice only Ron Halfshaft behaved as if

unaware of the gravity of the situation. Perhaps it was just his manner. He was like an enthusiastic student or academic pondering an abstract problem, not in touch with the grim reality.

He looked at his watch and smacked his lips. "Well, I don't know about you folks but I'm hungry. What I really need right now is a good American hamburger."

His remark broke the tension. "Shall we order in, or try the restaurant?" asked Carlton.

There was something intriguing about the idea of finding out how a Michelin starred restaurant would tackle a Big Mac and fries, so we voted to go and see.

Needless to say, the food when it came was excellent. I had ordered my hamburger rare, on hearing that it would be the best Charolais beef and I was not disappointed.

Disappointment was an emotion reserved for the waiter from whom Halfshaft ordered his burger well-done, but the man winced and complied.

One doesn't often find fries that surpass the MacDonalds version but there was something about these, they just melted in the mouth.

"How do they do that?" I asked of nobody in particular.

Carlton took the question seriously and beckoned the waiter, who nodded.

"Monsieur is probably tasting that our potatoes are fried in beef dripping. We understand MacDonalds no longer use beef fat but instead vegetable oil following a lawsuit by a Hindu customer."

He shrugged, banishing American culture to a culinary dustbin on the basis of this *horreur*.

Halfshaft was talking about his frustrating trip to the Casino de France, when he discovered they had no black-jack tables.

"So I sat through this weird ballet instead. I talked to this guy in the interval. He was kind of weird." He laughed.

Tisch shares with me a dislike of sloppy language. He looked at Halfshaft. "A weird evening, then?"

Halfshaft had no idea he was being teased.

"What was odd about the guy?" asked Mimi.

"I tried to chat but I could hardly get a word out of him."

She grinned. "That makes him weird?"

"Oh and he had this big suitcase which he stashed at the luggage counter. I saw him carrying it afterwards and it seemed really light, like it was empty."

Something bothered me about his story. As I sipped the glass of Bordeaux which I had favoured over a Coke, it came to me.

"Who did you say was going to perform at the Casino?"

He scratched his head. "Some broad. Christiane Rogers, maybe. Is it important?"

"It wasn't Christiane Rouget?"

"Yeah, that's it, Rouget."

"You know who she is?"

He grinned. "You got me." He stuffed the last of the fries

in his mouth, smacked his lips and took a long swig of Coca Cola.

"She happens to be the wife of Philippe Rouget, the Minister of the Interior."

"Good for her." He sounded at best half interested.

I said, "Here's a question. If you were going to blow up a building, how could you make an extra impact, reinforce the effect so to speak?"

Light began to dawn. Before he could speak, Carlton interrupted. "You may be onto something."

"I think so."

He nodded. "Nothing would generate headlines like the death of a major celebrity."

"From the political world."

"Check."

"Who is also glamorous."

"Check again."

"And you might rehearse by taking an empty bag there, representing the bomb, just to be sure that they would accept it at the left luggage counter."

Silence round the table.

"Did you notice when she is next performing there?" I asked Halfshaft. He shook his head.

"Take a look at the schedule."

The programmer borrowed Mimi's tablet and Googled the theatre's programme. After a few keystrokes, he looked up.

"She's performing in a couple of weeks time. At least that gives us some breathing space."

Then he did a double take. "No, wait. That doesn't include today's schedule."

He read the small type again. "It's tonight. She's singing tonight."

The breath almost left my body as I looked at the others. "If I'm right we only have a few hours to stop all hell breaking loose."

Carlton stood up. "That's where we need to be."

I said. "One of us, probably Mimi, should stay here as a message centre in case Kathy does call. The rest of us had better get moving."

"Should we alert the police?" asked Halfshaft.

Carlton shook his head. "I have a bad feeling about that. Oliver is right. If our man sees he is being hunted he'll make himself scarce, and fast."

"He hasn't met us personally, so we should not cause him alarm," I said.

"He's met me," said Halfshaft.

"That may not matter," I said. "You're just a harmless American he met in the bar."

"Let's go," said Tisch. He turned to me. "Bring your weapon."

I patted my pocket.

Minutes later we were crammed in a taxi heading for the Casino de France.

54

Kathy straightened up to find herself staring into the eyes of a mild looking man in his sixties who smiled politely.

"Nice little cars aren't they?" he said.

Her mind raced. He didn't look like a terrorist. And the license number was not the one she had been looking for. She tried to sound natural.

"Yes, I'm shopping for a new car, and I've been looking at this model of Fiat. They have been really well reviewed. I think reviews are important, don't you?"

She knew she was speaking too fast. The man's smile grew fixed. "Yes, you are doing the right thing. But why are you are paying such attention to the license plate?"

She felt herself blush. "No reason at all, really. I was just curious."

At that moment her phone rang and, reflexively, she answered it. It was Halfshaft.

The phone was set to loudspeaker by default so his voice was audible even above the passing cars, which was unfortunate. His first words were, "I'm thinking your man would live near a cash machine. He may have an account outside France with cashing privileges. It's difficult to do without one nowadays."

Halfshaft spoke with his usual brash enthusiasm. She stabbed at the phone to mute it and thrust it into a pocket of her jeans, but too late. The man had heard every word.

Zidane smiled. "Let's continue our chat in my apartment," he said. "As your clever friend guessed, it is nearby."

"I'd rather not. I'm pretty busy…"

But it was no use. His grip tightened and with a strength belying his appearance he manhandled her across the sidewalk, through a doorway and out of sight.

He dragged her, straining and resisting, up several flights. No good manners now. In moments she was in a small flat, pushed down on an upright chair in the kitchen, her wrists tied.

Kathy considered herself to be smart, alert and usually quick to react to adversity but the whole situation had developed too fast, and she was dazed. She glared at her captor.

"First things first," he said. He leaned forward. She had come out in tight jeans and tee shirt and carried no purse, just some folding money and her hotel key card. Her phone was in a front pocket. He teased the slim device out of her jeans with his hand and put it on the table. "If it rings I'll answer it for you."

She hoped it would not ring. The less he learned the better, either from her or her phone.

He stared at her for a moment, then got up and, walked over to the kitchen counter. He started to brew coffee, measuring the water into a shiny espresso machine followed by coffee from a can in the refrigerator. With much hissing and steaming, the machine delivered enough of the dark liquid to fill a small cup. Kathy, who did not have a sweet tooth, winced as he stirred in large amounts of sugar.

He came and sat opposite her, looking thoughtful.

"What should I make of you?" he asked.

"I was looking for a friend," she said. "I have no idea what you are doing but your conduct is beyond inexcusable. I might overlook your bad behaviour if you let me go, but I think you need to seek help."

She stared, trying to read his face. He was expressionless, so no luck there.

55

She watched Zidane pottering about the apartment - apart from the bathroom it was really just a large room with a bed in one corner and a kitchen in the other. The bomb in its innocent suitcase sat on the floor by the stove.

From her position tied to the chair she could see a second bag, a zip-up valise on the bed. Zidane seemed to be packing for a trip, methodically, almost fussily removing shirts and underwear from the chest of drawers and a suit from the hanging cupboard and stowing them neatly in the bag.

"Going far?" she asked.

"Yes, actually."

"Somewhere nice, I hope." Inane, but better than silence. It helped keep her spirits up.

He shook his head and went on with his work.

Kathy was at a loss. She didn't seem able to make any impression on this grey little man.

She cast about for ways to engage him. It crossed her mind to try and seduce him but he was so physically unexciting and the thought was so stomach-turning that she knew she couldn't possibly make a decent job of it, even if he were susceptible. He looked sexless she thought.

No, if she was to have any chance at all of distracting him, it had to be through some sort of reasoned appeal.

She did not expect to convert a lifelong fanatic with just a few clever arguments. That was absurd. But if she could just intrigue the man, engage him in a discussion, offer a better way of achieving his goal than killing thousands of people, perhaps she could bring about some kind of delay.

"We know what you're trying to do," she said.

He paused in his packing. "Do you?"

"Yes."

"What then?" A half smile.

"You're going to kill a lot of people with the device you have in that suitcase."

He nodded. "You seem to have learned a lot in a short time. Sadly for you, it comes too late."

"What are your plans?"

"I'm sorry, I don't have time to chat."

"Why are you doing this?" she asked desperately.

He looked at her. "Do you really want to know?"

He put down the things he was packing and came and

sat opposite her. "Have you heard of the Balfour Declaration?"

"The statement by the British government that led to the founding of Israel?"

"Yes. Also the worst example of corrupt, lying treachery in the history of politics.

"I would debate you but I'm not in a position to," she said, glancing at her bonds.

He went on. "Few people know that in addition to that promise, the British government made others. For example, they promised the Sharif of Mecca that the Arab movement would be guaranteed control of the Middle East."

She was geting out of her depth. Was any of this true, or just Zidane's own twisted version of history?

"With that declaration, the British caved in to pressure from the Jews. They thought it would undermine German Jewish support for Kaiser Wilhelm in 1917. At the time, many Jews supported the Kaiser and his policies, ironically in view of what happened in the Second World War.

"If that's true, surely you should blame the British, not the French? How does killing thousands of Frenchmen make sense?"

He sighed. "Young lady you are naive. My goal is the return of Palestine to the Palestine people. If you know anything about Middle Eastern politics you know that change does not happen through friendly discussion. Only force will change the world." He frowned. "I apply pressure. I apply force. The world will take notice."

His voice had risen and taken on an angry tone. He turned away and resumed his packing.

Well that worked well, she thought. "When will you be back?" she asked.

He considered the question. She thought it had taken him by surprise.

"Not tonight, in fact not for a while."

"What about me, then?"

She tried to sound calm but her voice quavered.

He turned and stared at her.

He was briefly at a loss. He had done some dreadful things, taken many lives and intended to do so again. But he usually managed to avoid face-to-face confrontation and he was not an experienced liar. He couldn't bring himself to tell this young woman that he had made no provision for her. She would remain tied to that chair until she died of hunger in an empty apartment.

"I shall arrange to have you released," he said.

"When?"

He hesitated. "Tomorrow."

"What time tomorrow?"

He turned away and continued packing. When he was finished, he opened the apartment door and placed both pieces of luggage on the landing outside. He left without looking at Kathy, closed the door and double locked it from the outside.

. . .

Mansour was waiting downstairs in the Peugeot. They drove first to Porte d'Italie Metro station in the far south of the 13th Arrondissement. It was six pm when they reached the station, just as planned, Zidane noted with satisfaction.

He left Mansour waiting with the car and the bag with his belongings. He bought a metro token and, carrying the suitcase with the bomb, boarded the train for Abbesses, the station nearest to the Casino.

He could not suppress a feeling of excitement as the train rumbled on its way. Everything was going according to plan.

The girl was a complication. But he had dealt with her. He did worry that she was not a lone operator, but, as time ticked by, his plans were coming so close to their climax that even if someone did manage to trace her, it would not matter.

So as he emerged from the station and approached the Casino, the sight of the American he had met a few days before, standing in the crowded lobby, did not dismay him. Nor did the look of agitation on the young man's face. It must be surprising for him too, after all.

Or so he thought. But moments later, Halfshaft's gaze fell to the suitcase in Zidane's hand and his expression turned to one of dismay.

Zidane knew then that he was in trouble. He had no idea why Halfshaft had appeared but it was one coincidence too many. The young American knew something. Zidane did not panic. His mind raced, telling him that his plan must change but he remained calm, even forcing a smile.

"Hello there," he said briskly. "We seem to have similar tastes in entertainment."

"Right," Halfshaft stammered. "I guess you came to hear Christiane Rouget?"

"That's why I'm here."

"Me too!" Halfshaft couldn't take his eyes off the suitcase. "You've brought your bag."

Zidane nodded. "I'm going on a trip later but I wanted to catch this show. Who knows when there will be another chance to hear Christiane – I understand her husband the Minister doesn't approve."

"Uh huh." It was more of a grunt than a reply. Halfshaft's self possession was rapidly deserting him.

"I must go and check this in," said Zidane. He moved towards the theatre cloakroom. As he passed Halfshaft, the suitcase brushed against the young American's leg.

Halfshaft leaped back as if he had received an electric shock.

The fool thinks it's going to explode, thought Zidane.

People turned and stared.

Halfshaft whirled and beckoned towards the street, shouting, "He's here!"

Of course, he would not be alone, Zidane thought. Flight was now his best option. If he could lose himself in the crowd he might still disappear and live to fight another day.

He almost succeeded. His appearance and dress were

ordinary, but the big suitcase got in the way – brown and heavy. He dared not leave it, but to thrust his way through the crowds, trundling it on its little wheels, was impossible with any speed.

He wanted to get back to the Metro; he saw over his shoulder that two more men were pushing their way through the throng, heading towards him. One looked vaguely familiar. They would surely catch him before he could reach the anonymity of the Metro station.

He paused at a crossroad controlled by traffic signals; there were cars waiting for the red light to change. A large black BMW driven by a woman in glasses stood at the head of the line of cars, waiting for the light to change. On an impulse he wrenched open the door and shoved his way violently into the driver's seat, displacing the woman who came to rest, bruised and startled, on the passenger side. He pulled the suitcase in after him and slammed the door.

The light turned green just then and he accelerated away.

56

I stumbled along in pursuit, cursing Halfshaft for his ineptness. If he had just walked over quietly and pointed to Zidane we could have nailed the guy right away. Still, spilt milk.

I caught intermittent glimpses of a slight figure in a fawn raincoat. Not conspicuous, but the suitcase was a giveaway. He was never going to part with that.

A black BMW was standing at the traffic lights and I saw him step towards the driver's door and yank it open. He jumped in just as the lights changed. I couldn't see inside, the windows were smoked glass, but the driver had to be totally flabbergasted. The license was one of those vanity plates, "SUE5BMW" – hardly the number of a terrorist.

Luckily there was a taxi to hand. I flagged it down, uttering the time-honoured words, "Follow that car!"

I pulled Tisch in with me but Halfshaft had fallen behind and we left him to fend for himself.

At first, we were a good hundred yards behind but our driver joined in the fun. He made good use of gaps in traffic and was soon only a couple of cars back from the BMW.

The lights of Paris were coming on in the dusk as we sped down Rue d'Amsterdam and Rue Tronchet before roaring through the Place de la Madeleine, across Place de la Concorde and hanging a hard right. We screamed along the north side of the river for about a mile before turning left towards Pont de l'Alma.

"Where the heck is this guy going?" Carlton muttered.

"I don't think he knows. He's just trying to shake us off."

Only a single car separated us as we approached the bridge but, at that point, rush hour congestion slowed everything to a halt.

As I watched, the BMW's window rolled down and an arm appeared with a gun. There was a crack and a bullet struck the road inches from our front wheels.

It was too much for our driver, who threw up his hands. I took that to mean that he was withdrawing his support. I couldn't really blame him.

"Hand me a pistol," I muttered to Carlton.

He put his Beretta in my hand. "The safety's off."

I leaned out and took aim at the arm and the gun. Traffic was not moving and I had good support for my arm. I thought I hit him. The arm disappeared. We watched for a second.

"What now?" asked Carlton.

"We get out."

Standing on the pavement yards from the BMW and its deadly driver, we were vulnerable and I knew it.

The door of the BMW opened slowly and a raincoat-clad figure stepped out, dragging the suitcase. Had I hit his gun arm? If so, with the suitcase, he had no good hand to hold a weapon.

He turned and started to cross the bridge at a shambling trot. It must have been difficult for him with the heavy suitcase and he slowed and stopped halfway across.

I trained the Beretta at the small of his back and approached. Twelve feet now – ten – eight.

"At this range, I can't miss," I said.

He turned and faced me.

The face was commonplace. Mousy hair receding at the temples. Glasses that looked as if they had thick lenses, an overall impression of greyness. His gaze flickered around looking for an option and, not seeing one, returned to my face. He nodded as if to say, it's your move.

"I'll take the suitcase, " I said.

"Ah, the suitcase." He looked at it in his hand. "It's quite valuable."

"And dangerous."

"When armed, certainly."

"Is it armed?"

"That would make a difference, no? If it is, and if I could disarm it, then I would have bargaining power."

"I don't think it's armed," I said.

He shrugged, and smiled.

We stood and looked at each other. My gun was trained on his stomach now.

"If I shoot it will be painful," I said quietly.

He was close to the waist-high balustrade. He turned and hoisted the suitcase up onto the railing. He held it, resting but tilted away, one hand preventing it from falling.

"If you shoot me you'll never know," he said.

The decision was taken away from us because the railing was slicker than he realised and the suitcase was starting to slide away. Before he could strengthen his grip it disappeared into the night against a backdrop of the floodlit Eiffel Tower.

He turned and faced me unencumbered. I was taking no chances. I moved forward quickly and jammed the Beretta in his midriff. I found his automatic and put it in my own pocket.

"So are we all going to be vaporised?" I asked.

He shook his head. "You were right, it wasn't armed."

"Well that's something at least,"

He smiled. "Are you going to deliver me to the police?"

I had visions of him cheating justice by biting a suicide capsule, or some such method. I wanted him to live, at least for a while.

"That depends," I said.

57

T isch had not said much during the pursuit. It had been pretty strenuous and he was not a young man. But now that it was over he had a chance to look at Zidane and what he saw chilled him.

He knew the man's history: he had been responsible over the years for many bomb attacks against Jews in Europe and the Middle East. His stated goal was to promote Palestine as an Arab state – no pusillanimous two-state solution for Zidane. For him, it was death to every last Jew.

It was hard to associate the inoffensive looking character in the raincoat with the dreadful things he had done. Tisch wondered how a normal looking person could be so odious. And this was an adult, not a weak minded youngster radicalised by the raving of some extremist imam. He must have reflected on what he was doing. He must know that the political dividend from his acts was questionable, yet he was still at work causing havoc. What was he made of?

Tisch did not pretend to be objective. His own relatives had perished in the Holocaust. When he heard stories of the camps: starvation, forced marches, mass graves, he felt not just grief but fear, cold and gut-wrenching. A different turn of events and that would have been him.

It made the small figure before him an object not of dislike but of loathing.

With an effort, he preserved a calm expression and nodded at Oliver. "Good work. Let's turn him in."

"Not just yet," said Oliver.

58

We returned to the taxi.

The driver had been tipped 200 euros by Carlton, probably the most the man had ever earned for a fifteen minute ride, so he was still more or less on board, but he was clearly unnerved by the gunfire. When he saw me holding the Beretta in Zidane's ribs he rolled his eyes.

"Where now?" he asked.

"That depends on our fellow passenger here."

I turned to Zidane. "You are holding a young woman called Kathy Smith. We want her released."

"I have no idea what you are talking about."

"Really? I think you do. And now that the bomb is at the bottom of the Seine, we might consider letting you go if you help us on this."

He shook his head.

I wound down the cab window and a blast of cool air blew in. I raised the Beretta and pointed it at his head.

Would I have pulled the trigger? Possibly. But Zidane thought for a second, then spoke to the driver.

"You can go to Rue du Parc-de-Montien."

The driver looked at me and I nodded.

The trip took twenty minutes. We stopped outside an entry door next to a grocery store.

"Welcome to my modest home," said Zidane.

We got out. I was keeping Zidane covered. Carlton had his Beretta out and was doing the same. We knew that it was last chance time for the terrorist and he would be desperate.

"Do you want to wait?" I asked the driver. "We'll be back in a few minutes."

It took him a millisecond to decide. "Thanks, but I think I'll move on. It's been interesting, but..."

He drove away, burning rubber.

We approached the door and Zidane produced a key.

"Which floor?" asked Carlton.

"The fourth."

"No elevator?"

Zidane shook his head. He seemed to have little regard for Carlton, perhaps because I had done most of the talking.

Four flights later it was Zidane who was breathing heavily. He was somewhere north of sixty, I reminded myself, not that that entitled him to any sympathy.

He let us in.

"What kept you so long?" said Kathy from the floor.

She had rocked the chair to and fro until it had fallen over, dumping her on the thin carpet, but she was basically unhurt. I untied her and Carlton brought her a glass of water. Then, while I kept Zidane covered, Carlton used the same bonds to tie the terrorist's wrists firmly behind his back.

"So where's the bomb?" asked Kathy.

"At the bottom of the river," I said.

She put her arms around me and burst into tears.

Zidane stood in the corner, watching.

"Now," he said, "You promised you would consider releasing me."

"So we did," I said. I looked at Carlton.

"I've considered it," I said.

"So have I," said Carlton.

We both shook our heads.

"Sorry," I said. "But I'm afraid we'll have to turn you in. We did promise the French and the way things are, what with Charlie Hebdo . . ."

Zidane shrugged. He didn't seem surprised.

"One more thing," said Carlton.

He walked over to Zidane, took careful aim, and shot him in the knee.

"That's for Katerina," he said.

Sometimes you think you know people, then you find out you don't know them very well at all.

.   .   .

Next morning, we went to the Préfecture for a wrap up with the Prefect.

A couple of his deputies were there. We sat at one end of the huge conference table, admiring the chandeliers.

"We're very grateful," said Villeneuve. "When we got your call last night, our people went to the apartment and found Zidane, just as you said. A terrible disaster avoided and a terrorist captured who we have been pursuing for years. Quite a day!"

A deputy leaned across and whispered in his ear. Villeneuve frowned, then looked over at me.

"I wasn't aware that Zidane had been shot in the knee."

"Yes, he was."

"How did that happen?"

"He was trying to escape," said Tisch.

The Frenchmen all turned and looked at him.

"Can you tell us a bit more?" asked Villeneuve. "It was a nasty wound."

Tisch shook his head. "He was trying to escape."

"With what firearm was he shot?"

Tisch was silent. After a while it became clear that he had no intention of saying anything more.

Villeneuve coughed and looked at his watch. "Well I think that concludes our business."

Smiles and handshakes all round. Very polite, the French. Most of the time.

. . .

Back at the Meurice, Mimi took me aside." Are you two sleeping together?" she asked.

"Excuse me? We're good friends," I said, trying to sound light. Was it any of her business?

"If you're sleeping together my dear, good luck to you both. You're both free white and twenty-one. But don't you dare hurt her, do you hear?"

That had not occurred to me. More the other way around.

"Men can be vulnerable too," I said.

"Rubbish," said Mimi.

59

I tried to concentrate on planning my journey back to England the next day but for some reason my thoughts kept being distracted by mental pictures of Kathy.

My mind was increasingly preoccupied by the relationship. In fact, I was in a state of barely controlled exhilaration over the way things had developed in recent weeks.

We seemed to be getting on well and the physical side was electric, no doubt about that. But how did she really feel about me? That was harder to gauge.

I couldn't read her. She didn't conform to any of the usual feminine stereotypes. No disrespect to the romantic ideal and its distinguished place in the spectrum of womanhood, but she just wasn't it. Too quirky, too complex and a bit political.

What was I to her? Lover, business colleague, boy-toy or some combination of the above? I would not have been ashamed to be classified as any of those but it would be nice to know which.

It dawned on me that, either way, I was in the grip of a full-fledged addiction but somehow I didn't mind. It was a good addiction.

60

November 12th, 2015

Next morning, I woke up early, before Kathy. I was shaving when I saw her in the bathroom mirror. She looked relaxed and sleepy. "Hi," I said.

We took a shower. The tub was not huge but the shower head was one of those wide ones almost a foot across that you get in hotels sometimes and we were quite happy staying close anyway, so it didn't matter. We lathered each other comprehensively, nothing overlooked. Eventually, we patted one another dry with the fluffy white towels before collecting our clothes from the floor where they had ended up the night before.

I looked in my suitcase. Better try and dress a bit

smarter I thought, with her here. Then I thought, damn, this episode is ending, she won't be around tomorrow.

It was leaving time. We walked to the lobby.

She said, "I'm flying to Tortola, spend a few days. Play some tennis with Mimi."

"Sounds like fun."

"Are you going back to Chelsea?" she asked.

"Yes, I am."

"You should go somewhere different. London gets so cold."

"Maybe I will. I've been meaning to go to Cuba."

"That sounds interesting."

"Would you come with me?" I asked. "For a vacation. We could be tourists together."

A pause, then she said, "I don't want to answer that here. Not in Paris. You'll miss your train. Go!"

I kissed her and got in the taxi and said "Gare du Nord," and the taxi drove off.

It was November 12th.

61

Two days later

Rashid Mirza and his colleague Aziz were drinking beer in the bar of the Islamabad Club after a hard game of squash.

Earlier the two engineers had watched reports of the bloody slaughter at the Bataclan concert hall in Paris the day before.

Munir Chaudry had telephoned from Paris to tell them about the debacle involving their own bomb, which had received no publicity. Zidane was in prison, Chaudry himself was under investigation. The unarmed device was at the bottom of the Seine.

They were disappointed but not heartbroken – they could always build another bomb, and faster this time with the experience they had gained. And they had been paid.

Mirza had a warm feeling when he thought about his Swiss bank account.

They did regret losing a real-life field test. Zidane's project would have provided proof of fitness for purpose that, for obvious reasons, could not be otherwise arranged.

"What next?" asked Aziz.

Aziz was the aggressive one – Mirza had always been more intrigued by the challenge of building the device, although the money was important.

Mirza shrugged. "We get on with our day jobs."

His cell phone rang and he answered it. As he listened, his expression changed from surprise to annoyance. Finally, he spoke. "Yes, we could meet. No, I could not bring one with me, they are complex items."

The voice on the line got louder and Mirza put down the phone.

"Well?" asked Aziz.

"That was an associate of Mullah Saddiq."

Saddiq was a militant Al Qaeda leader, believed to be living somewhere in the mountains.

"What did he want?"

"He wants a small nuclear device."

"I wonder if that's a good idea," said Aziz.

"He said they won't take no for an answer."

THE END

Now read on for a sneak peek at the next *Oliver Steele and Kon Feaver* thriller, *CASINO HAVANA*:

GRAHAM
TEMPEST

CASINO HAVANA

Chapter 1

I stood gazing out to sea from the Malecon in Havana, the great sweeping four-mile promenade facing the ocean.

In front of me were the Florida Straits and ninety miles away, below the horizon, Key West and the United States. Behind me, the handsome but weary buildings of Havana.

Haunting my thoughts was my old friend Kon Feaver, rotting in a Cuban jail. My task: to rescue him.

The chances of success: not great.

Chapter 2

Three days earlier I had been relaxing on the *Plage de Tahiti* at Saint-Tropez, topless capital of the world.

Kathy and I had spent the previous week in Paris. We helped prevent a terrorist from vaporising the city with a small atom bomb, so you could say we were in celebration mode.

I had taken a taxi to the Gare du Nord to return to London but then annoyed the driver by asking him to turn around and take me back to the Hotel Meurice.

Kathy and Mimi were having tea in the elegant Dali Room. Mimi is an ex-Playboy centrefold. She's also the twenty-five year old third wife of my biggest client, sixty year old Carlton Tisch.

I envy Carlton both for his millions and for his wife but my main interest is in Mimi's friend, Kathy.

Mimi smiled. "Hi, what's up?"

"Where's Carlton?" I really just wanted to see Kathy again.

"He's working."

"What are you ladies up to?"

They looked at each other. "We're going to the Riviera for a few days," said Mimi.

"Saint-Tropez," said Kathy. "We're in France, after all."

Mimi and Kathy are the same age and the same height and build. Both are knockouts by any standard. Mimi is dark haired and Kathy blonde but they could be sisters.

They share a waspish sense of humour, meaning they discuss people behind their backs with relish. 'People' includes me. Their closeness has led some to suggest there's something physical going on and I wonder about that, but if so they are discreet about it. Both have relationships with men – Mimi with her husband and Kathy with me.

"Come too," said Mimi. "Carlton has to fly home but Mike Kalestian is in town. He may join us."

Kalestian is a friend of Carlton's but younger, about thirty-five. He owns casinos in Las Vegas and Macau. He's a brash bounder with flashing eyes and a big moustache who works out and wears Speedos. I don't like him.

I rubbed my chin. "Not sure I can spare the time."

"Go on," said Mimi. "It'll be fun."

So after much deliberation I found room in my busy schedule.

Chapter 3

"I'm not looking forward to being ogled by Kalestian the Speedo king," said Kathy.

We were in a small hotel down by Saint-Tropez Harbour, in a room overlooking the fishing boats.

Besides being cute Kathy is sharp witted, more so than me, which is a turn-on. She also speaks her mind. I've been told I'm prejudiced in favour of strong women. Guilty as charged. She's five foot seven and nicely rounded, with gleaming fair hair, a tee shirt and jeans person, not *haute couture*.

"You don't like him, do you?" she said.

"No."

She sat at the dressing table combing her blonde hair, wet from the shower. She had teamed up tee shirt-wise with Superbowl winner Tom Brady. Tom's handsome mug beamed from a 100% pre-shrunk cotton number that did nothing to cover her legs.

"You have great legs," I said.

"I do, don't I," she said.

Chapter 4

At the beach we undressed down to our swimsuits. Kathy's white bikini offset her golden tan.

"Keep going," I said.

She gave me a look between amused and annoyed and peeled off her bra.

Mimi hesitated which was interesting because before she married Carlton she had posed for a Playboy spread that went well beyond topless, but she followed suit.

Once we were oiled and sipping our drinks, Kalestian asked me, "Where's your friend Kon?"

"Florida. He had a run to make."

"A run?"

"To Cuba."

Kon is a free spirit who runs a boat service from Cuba to Florida for refugees who want to make a new life in the United States. He keeps a sturdy forty foot cruiser at his home on Coquina Key. His knowledge of the lonely stretch of islands and causeways running from Key Largo to Key West makes him a formidable guide.

"So he's a coyote?" asked Kalestian. He used the derogatory term for a people smuggler.

"Absolutely not," said Kathy. "Coyotes take huge fees. Kon just charges for gas plus something to live on."

Mimi's mobile phone rang.

"Hi Carlton," she said.

"Hold on."

She handed me the phone. "Speak of the devil. It's about Kon."

"Hi, Carlton."

"Kon's been arrested."

I was shocked and also surprised. It was true that smuggling people was illegal in both Cuba and the United States but Cuba was not as concerned as it once was about refugees. And at the U.S. end, Kon was adept at finding remote spots in the Keys to unload his passengers, so his risk of being caught there was minimal.

"How serious is it?"

"He's in a Cuban jail."

"How come?"

"We're trying to find out. I guess there was a tipoff because when Kon got to the pickup point the Cuban police were there in force."

"Is he okay?"

A pause. "Bruno thinks he was badly beaten up." Bruno was Kon's contact in Havana.

That was the end of my Riviera vacation. The accountant in me said I should finish my spell at the beach and then return to my home in Coconut Grove to await news. But I just couldn't.

Kon is a good friend, although he's about as different from me as a person can be. He's a genial ex-Israeli fighter pilot and recovering alcoholic who played soccer for Tel Aviv, was tossed out of the Israeli Air Force for excessive drinking and then roamed the world as a mercenary before getting into people-smuggling.

I by contrast am an accountant, the product of a pricy

British education, not noted for my wide emotional range. I'm not ashamed of that, in fact I'm proud of it.

So Kon and I are polar opposites.

But I had to help him.

Chapter 5

"Why were you carrying Sanchez Madera?"

In Cienfuegos, Cuba, sometimes known as the Pearl of the South, an individual with a scarred face and a personality to match stood in front of Kon Feaver, who was tied to a chair.

Kon spat out a tooth. "Who's Sanchez Madera?"

"He was waiting to board your boat."

"I don't know anything about that."

The man punched him savagely in the stomach.

Chapter 6

In his office in Cienfuegos, Police Commander Hector Cruz was reading the Miami Herald on his laptop.

The 'phone rang.

"Yes?"

"This is Marco. We're getting nowhere with the American."

"I told you not to use that term."

"The prisoner then."

"What's the problem?"

"He's very stubborn."

"You may have to put him in *la caja*."

There was a pause. "I don't know if that'll work. It's a slow process and you said you wanted quick results."

Cruz's black hair shone with gel. He was pale skinned and his short black beard was trimmed to a point. His otherwise handsome face was marred by a permanent frown.

He wore the blue and grey uniform of an officer in the PNR, the Policía Nacional Revolucionaria. The uniform looked drab on most people but on his muscular frame the neatly pressed grey shirt with epaulettes and badges of rank on the shoulders was quite flattering.

The senior officer in a police territory covering two provinces, at the age of forty his clean-cut looks and humourless manner had served him well as a fast-rising star – he came across as a dedicated agent of the state who would enforce the law without pity.

La caja – the box – was a tiny cell four feet square and

three feet high in which it was impossible to stand or sit in comfort. After a few hours the pain in the subject's limbs and joints became intense. He would twist and turn in a futile attempt at relief. Prisoners were often left there for weeks in extreme heat with minimal slops for food and no toilet. Occasionally the door would be opened briefly to sluice the subject down and remove the dirt and excrement.

"Put him there anyway. It'll soften him up." He went back to reading about Cuba's First Vice President, Miguel Díaz-Canel.

The uncensored availability of the Herald, no supporter of the Castros, reflected the changing times. Since Fidel turned the presidency over to his brother Raul, things had relaxed slightly. Raul, eighty-five himself, had indicated he would not run for office in 2018, so this was a sort of interim period, post-Fidel and pre . . . pre what, exactly?

That was the question. What did the next few years hold? And among the ambitious, who would advance?

Raul's pending retirement had turned the spotlight on Díaz-Canel, an engineer by training and supposedly progressive. The man had played his cards well, thought Cruz cynically. He had managed not to be perceived as a rival to the Castros, unlike other contenders now in prison or dead, so he seemed well placed to succeed to the presidency.

But not if Cruz had anything to do with it. He was thir-teen years younger than the vice president. That meant that, unless he could jump ahead, he was in for a long wait. Some would have been content to wait their turn but not Cruz.

He finished reading and switched off the computer.

He had been successful so far, which was reflected in his surroundings. The house was built in the 1920's as the beach home of a wealthy sugar growing family but was confiscated when Castro took power. The second floor room was spacious, its wood floor waxed until it gleamed, paintings by modern Cuban artists Rafael Martinez and Wilfredo Lam lining the walls.

But past success was not enough. The rest of his plan must be executed rigorously. And one of Kon Feaver's passengers was a major threat to that plan.

Chapter 7

After speaking to Cruz, the jailer Marco beckoned to an associate and together they left the small concrete block cabin that served as an office and strolled across the sand to the prison yard.

Cayo Piedra was a prison island. Few Cubans even knew of its existence.

The island was barely a mile long. The prison consisted of two single storey buildings, each with a dozen cells, standing on opposite sides of a square. The yard was bordered by a twenty foot high chain link fence topped with razor wire. In the centre was a watchtower tall enough for the guards to overlook both cell blocks.

A couple of guards lounged in the tower, rifles slung from their shoulders. When they saw Marco emerge from the office outside the fence they straightened up and one of them came down to let him and his companion into the compound.

Marco did not show much sense of caution. He was unarmed. Only a few cells were occupied. In the entire life of the prison there had never been a successful escape, such was the remoteness of the island and the brutality with which occasional attempts were punished.

One such punishment was about to be applied. They approached a cell, unlocked it and went inside.

Chapter 8

"Get him up," said Marco.

Kon was sitting on the earth floor with his back propped against the wall. He was hungry and thirsty and his face was a mess of cuts and bruises. The midday heat was overpowering with no breeze to cool the cells. He had little reason for hope of rescue or even easy treatment so his spirits were low but when he heard the key turn and saw the door open, he determined not to show it and straightened up slightly.

The guard pulled Kon upright.

The Israeli could barely stand unaided. He wiped blood and sweat from his face.

"I'll ask again," said Marco. "Why were you carrying Sanchez Madera?" His English was crude and accented but his voice was calm, almost sympathetic.

"I told you, I have no idea. He was someone who paid for a place on my boat, nothing more. I don't ask about the personal lives of my passengers."

Marco shook his head sadly. He motioned to the guard. "Take him."

He returned to his office, and telephoned Cruz.

"He's in *la caja*. But his attitude is poor. Don't expect quick results."

At the other end of the line, Cruz grunted and hung up. He stared out of the window, thought for a moment and then telephoned a number in the United States.

Chapter 9

The mobile phone rang in the pocket of Stanley Rothman, in a top floor conference room at the massive Portofino Resort in Las Vegas.

"It's Cruz, Mr. Rothman."

"What d'you want?" Rothman's voice was gruff. He excused himself and walked out onto the balcony for privacy. It was quiet there apart from the low hum of traffic on Las Vegas Boulevard far below.

"We're sweating the prisoner to learn more about Sanchez Madera."

"Will that work?"

"It always does eventually."

"Keep me posted."

"Yes, sir."

Cruz's tone was respectful, reflecting the unequal relationship. He was a supplicant deferring to his backer. Rothman owned the Portofino, along with its clone in Macau and several other casinos.

He was in the middle of a meeting with Diana Jacobs, a partner in the accounting firm that audited his business. They were discussing the company's financial statements.

He was a short man in his early eighties. There was a carefully cultivated spring in his step but tell-tale signs – the red in his thin hair fighting a losing battle with the grey, and large liver spots on his pale forehead – gave the game away. Even in the sunshine he wore a suit with the jacket buttoned against chills. He went back inside.

"Well, Madam Auditor, what's your bottom line?"

She smiled. She was well aware that Rothman, who she found repulsive, still fancied himself a ladies man. Her youth and good looks had been factors in her company assigning her this account and she felt she should be liberal with her flattery. "You made a lot of money last year."

He frowned. "Save the compliments my dear, what I pay you for is frank advice."

"Fair enough. Then let me point out some areas of concern."

"Go ahead."

"Your Macau casino is profitable but this handsome resort here in Las Vegas barely breaks even."

Rothman nodded. "Go on."

"It's not alone, of course. Half the resorts on the Strip are in the same boat."

"How do I fix that?"

"I'm not sure you can."

"Raise prices?"

She shook her head. "Too much competition. Casinos on Indian land. Internet gambling. And prices here already reflect that today's Las Vegas is a luxury destination."

Rothman nodded. "That's why I invested in Macau."

"Which has bailed you out handsomely."

"Yes, it's been a cash cow."

"Long may that last," said Jacobs.

But there was a fly in the ointment and they both knew it. Much of Macau's early profits had come from criminals laundering their illegal income. Then China's anticorruption President Xi Jinping cracked down and cash flow fell off dramatically.

"You're going to need another trick soon," said Jacobs.

"I may have one."

"Really?"

Rothman nodded. "That call I just took was from Cuba. What if I told you that one day soon there will be casinos in Havana again and I shall be the biggest investor there?"

Jacobs looked doubtful. She recognised the exotic appeal of the island nation and Havana's gaudy history as a gaming mecca pre-Castro, with tales of the Mafia, prostitution and high life. But those days were long gone. True, relations with the United States had eased recently but the boycott was still in place. The prospect of U.S. investment in casinos, an industry forbidden fifty years ago under Castro was, in her private opinion, a pipe dream.

"Do you see things changing?" she asked.

"Yes. And when they do I shall have an inside track."

"How so?"

"I'm financing the next President of Cuba."

Chapter 10

I called my boss Carlton Tisch in New York.

"What's happening?" he asked.

"I don't really know where to start," I said.

He was in his so-called office – an elegant townhouse on East 62nd Street – having breakfast at the mahogany dining table, the one that magically turned into a conference table if the IRS threatened to visit.

A word about Carlton. He's a grumpy piece of work who doesn't suffer fools gladly. He started with nothing and is now worth north of a billion dollars. His parents ran a small deli on the Lower East Side and there was no college money for young Carl, but he got a job in the mail room at Goldman Sachs. Within a year he persuaded Goldman to back the takeover of an ailing debt finance company with himself as president. Talk about hustle. He now owns Eastern Debt Factors, the largest firm of its kind in the eastern states.

He's slow to put his hand in his pocket when it comes time to pay for a round but he's not as mean as he likes to pretend. I've seen his tax returns and the amount he gives to charity every year is more than I earn in a decade.

Carlton and Kon Feaver go back a long way. He trusts Kon. When he doesn't want to admit ownership of some fishy venture he puts it in Kon's name. There's no formal contract, just trust. Divorce lawyers for both his ex-wives attest to the power of the arrangement.

"Call Kon's contact in Havana, this guy Bruno," he snapped. "That's who I spoke to."

Bruno is a fixer. He's useful to Kon at the Cuban end, lining up passengers. Kon likes him but doesn't trust him.

I phoned Bruno. The line from Saint-Tropez was surprisingly clear.

"Bruno, this is Oliver Steele, a friend of Kon."

"Hi, Mr. Oliver."

"Just Oliver. What happened that night? Were you there?"

"Yes, but truly Mr. Oliver, I could not prevent it."

"Just Oliver, Bruno. It's okay, we're not blaming you. Tell me what happened."

"We were at a beach in Matanzas, twenty kilometres east of Havana."

I had the map of Cuba open on my laptop. Matanzas was shown in black capitals, a province somewhat east of Havana. I switched to Wikipedia.

"I see Matanzas. Apparently it has excellent beaches."

"That's why we use it. There's a place where Kon can bring his boat close to the shore. He uses a rubber dinghy to transfer the passengers."

"What's your part in the process?"

"I monitor the weather – the operation needs a calm night and no moon. I also assemble the passengers, usually between six and twenty people, and bring them from Havana in my van."

"You have a place in Havana?"

"Yes. It's a house I use for . . ." He paused.

"For what?"

"Another business."

Bruno ran a black market warehouse. If you needed a toaster that cost thirty dollars in the States, Bruno would sell it to you for fifty, but you would be lucky to find one at all in a government store. People like Bruno were a significant part of the Cuban economy, acting as a bridge between the needs of the individual and a state system that fell way short of meeting them. But if he wanted to be coy about how he made a living, okay.

"Go on," I said.

"That evening, the passengers found their way to my office in Havana as usual. I put them in the van and drove to Matanzas."

"How much did you know about them?"

"I knew their money was good."

"I thought nobody had money in Cuba. How did they pay?"

"Some had CUPs, some had CUCs. Others paid in dollars."

CUPs and CUCs were the two parallel currencies used in Cuba. CUP meant the Cuban peso and CUC the convertible peso, tied to the dollar. It's an awkward system that Fidel introduced in the nineties to preserve precious hard currency.

"Dollars? You have a dollar account?"

He hesitated. "Not in Cuba. I have an arrangement in . . . another place."

I guessed he meant a Caribbean tax haven – possibly Tortola where Carlton lived, or the Caymans. Grand Cayman, about two hundred miles south of Cuba would be a convenient choice for someone with a boat. My understanding of Bruno's grey netherworld was broadening.

"What happened then?"

"Once in Matanzas I drove out along the coast road to our beach. It was a calm evening as I said, no moon. Kon was coming from Florida, we had arranged to meet at nine. He's a good seaman and usually punctual.

"Things seemed fine at first. The passengers were waiting, each with one bag like on the airlines. Kon's boat arrived, without lights and moving as quietly as possible. It dropped anchor – he uses a light anchor but it bites into the sand pretty well – and he pushed the inflatable raft over the side.

"He was loading the first passengers when things went crazy. A large launch roared in, its searchlight sweeping around. It blocked Kon's boat from getting away. A bunch of uniformed men emerged from the bushes."

"Armed?"

"Of course."

"What were they – police, coastguard?"

"They were PNR."

"PNR?"

"Policia Nacional Revolucionaria. The regular police. You could see their uniforms in the glare – grey shirts and blue trousers, standard police kit."

"Whereabouts were you?"

"I was in my van."

"What did you do?"

"I slid down in the seat, hoping not to be seen. But a sergeant came and hauled me out of there."

"How come you are here to tell the tale?"

He shrugged. "They let me go. It sounds odd, I know. But smuggling people out of Cuba is not a huge deal nowadays. They book you, of course, and you have to go to court. For a first offence you probably get a warning and pay a fine."

"Is that all?"

"Sure. I don't think they care. If a few people make it across the Straits and reach dry land, so what? Once they get settled, they will send dollars back to their families in Cuba. Everybody wins."

"That's why this raid is surprising. Why all the drama?" I asked.

"Beats me." He didn't sound too interested.

"Doesn't it suggest they were looking for somebody? Not Kon, someone else?"

"Maybe."

"It also sounds as if they expected you guys would be there."

"I guess."

"How could they have known that?" I asked.

"Maybe somebody tipped them off."

"How could that happen?"

"I don't know. It wasn't me."

"What happened then?"

"The passengers scattered. They were trying to get away. They ran in all directions. The police chased them and here's the thing: they caught all but one of them. Out of six passengers they caught five and brought them back. One guy got away."

"Smart of him."

"Yeah, but there were a lot of sand dunes and a lot of bushes. And the ocean itself, perhaps he just swam out to sea. Maybe he drowned. Whatever, they didn't catch him. And they were pretty mad when they came back, so he could be the one you're talking about, the one they really wanted."

"What was his name?"

"Martin. A college professor, I think. Like I say, they didn't get him."

I tried to discern a trail I could follow. "This Martin. How did he pay?"

"In dollars."

"From where?"

Bruno hesitated as if not understanding. "I forget."

"You must have records."

"Just a minute." Sounding cross he left the phone and came back a minute later. "I received wired funds from the Bank of A. Spiro on Tortola."

The name rang a bell. Spiro was a small bank but I knew of it and had used it occasionally. It was known for flexibility. Carlton Tisch had done business with them too and he handled much bigger bucks than I, so we might have an introduction there.

"Does it mention the sender's name?"

"No. Just the amount, five thousand dollars."

"Five thousand? Kon charges much less."

I knew Kon only charged his passengers three thousand, far below the market rate for people-smuggling, a business which traditionally gouged passengers for every last penny. The going rate was twelve grand. I could have dropped the matter, but annoyance got the better of me.

He sounded whiny. "I have expenses. And the risk is great."

I didn't want to start a fight. It was more important to find Kon. "Go on."

"It was odd. Why the police? The Coastguard I could understand, but the police?"

"Here's a theory," I said. "Someone had it in for this guy Martin but didn't want folk to see what they were up to, so they planned this raid on their own. They set you free because they didn't want it becoming a news item. They wanted things kept quiet."

"So it wasn't a real government operation? But the police were there!"

"It could have been planned by someone in the police who had a private agenda."

"What sort of agenda?"

"Who knows? Financial, political, a mixture?"

"Beats me, buddy," he said.

I nodded although he couldn't see me. "Damn right, buddy."

Chapter 11

I called Tisch again.

"Bruno doesn't know where Kon is but he gave me a lead to a guy who was involved in the raid and got away. He paid his passage with a draft from the Bank of A. Spiro."

Tisch laughed. "Honest Abe!"

"You use him, don't you?"

"Not lately. Abe Spiro will do anything if the price is right."

"Oh dear me."

"Don't be cute," said Tisch. "I prefer to do business with people with impeccable ethics."

"Nowadays," I said.

"What's that supposed to mean?"

"Sounds like the old businessman's motto: Get on, get honour, get honest."

Tisch has a sense of humour, he's too smart not to, but I wouldn't call it elastic. "What do you need from me?" he snapped.

"An introduction to Spiro. I want to know who paid for the mystery man's passage to Florida. You have leverage so please call him. You can let him think there's some business coming his way."

"What sort of business?"

"I don't know. How about a fat foreign exchange transaction at his standard commission?"

"Forget it. He would want one percent and I never pay above a quarter."

"You needn't do it, just say you're thinking about it."

"I'll think about it."

Chapter 12

Apparently Carlton was able to bend his moral code because Abe Spiro greeted me like a long lost friend.

Which was just as well because when I walked into his comfortable office in Road Town I was pretty groggy. I had flown from Paris via London to Antigua which alone took sixteen hours. The plane was late reaching Antigua, so I missed the connecting flight to Tortola. I caught the ferry to Soper's Hole instead, rented a Jeep and, half awake, negotiated Tortola's corkscrew goat paths across the island trying hard not to drive off the road.

Spiro was tanned and grey haired, pushing seventy, and wore a crisp white shirt and a Haileybury tie. He shook my hand vigorously and poured us each a gin and tonic.

He spoke perfect BBC English.

"For some reason I thought you were American," I said.

He laughed and shook his head. "English and Greek. Born and raised in Hampstead. My wife's American, maybe that's what you had in mind. My father-in-law set me up in the banking business. I still do the odd deal but I'm semi-retired. I sail, play a bit of squash and generally enjoy island life."

I explained about Kon. "I'm short of leads. I want to learn more about this character Martin who is on the run from the Cuban police."

Spiro blinked but he made no bones about it. He pulled out the records and studied them.

"His name is Martin Sanchez Madera. He's actually

rather a fine person. He's an academic but also a frustrated journalist and politician. Neither of which are good things to be in Cuba unless you admire the Castros, which he does not. I don't know why he was on your friend's boat but it probably had something to do with his commitment to restoring democracy in Cuba."

"How are you involved?"

"When I'm in Miami I play golf with Pedro Macias, the son of Hugo."

I recognised the names. The older Macias was a freedom fighter with Fidel Castro but disapproved of Castro's turn to communism. Fidel arrested him and threw him in prison for twenty years for betraying the revolution – the usual excuse. After years of torture and privation Macias sought exile in Florida and was now prominent in the émigré community.

"Do you do business with Pedro?"

"We do a few deals, mostly real estate. Two years ago he asked me to open an account for Sanchez Madera. The funds came from the Macias family so presumably Hugo and Pedro Macias support Martin's political activity."

"I would think so."

"Pedro, particularly, is active in Cuban affairs."

"What does that mean?"

"Fund raising, public speaking. There are also rumours . . . " He hesitated.

"Rumours?"

"That he is training commandos in the Everglades."

"With a view to what? Not another invasion, surely? The Bay of Pigs was a fiasco, both military and political."

"Who knows?"

I filed that away for future reference.

"By the way," he said, "Carlton knows the Macias family. You should get him to arrange a meeting."

I got up to leave. "Thanks, you've been really helpful."

He shrugged. "I know I broke a confidence but, if Martin is in trouble, what you're doing may help him."

"You will be rewarded," I said. "Carlton talked about sending some business your way."

He smiled. "I won't hold my breath. Carlton's a great guy but I know a come-on when I hear one. You can't kid a kidder."

I called Tisch in Miami. "You never said you knew Pedro Macias."

"I know a lot of people."

"I want to meet him."

He thought briefly. "Lunch tomorrow. The Forge on Miami Beach."

Carlton can move fast when he wants to, which is fine but it meant more travelling for me.

Chapter 13

"Just hold on," Kon told himself in *la caja*.

He had been unconscious. He had no idea how many hours he had been in the box but it was growing dark now and it had been the middle of the day when they shut him in. His eyes had grown accustomed to the gloom – a few cracks admitted faint light. The heat, overpowering at first, was still intense.

His head ached and his face felt flushed. He wondered if his body temperature was climbing. He had read somewhere that heat stroke occurred when your temperature rose to a certain level and went on rising at an accelerating rate; it was fatal if not addressed in time. The treatment was to wrap you in ice and spray you with freezing water. Fat chance of that happening here.

He grunted in pain as his legs spasmed with piercing cramps. The muscles in his knotted calves felt as if they were being stretched to snapping point and it was all he could do not to scream. Lying on his side in a semi-foetal position, he tried to stretch but banged his feet on the wooden sides of the box. It was like being in a coffin, a comparison he tried to dismiss – there was an ominous finality to the thought.

The cramps passed after what felt like minutes but was probably just a few seconds. He knew they would come back, and worse because of the dehydration.

His spine ached, something separate. It felt like hot irons clamped to the small of his back. Nothing 600 milligrams of Ibuprofen wouldn't fix, he thought drily.

At some point he lost consciousness again.

*To buy **CASINO HAVANA,** go to GrahamTempest.com or to the bookstore or website where you bought this book*

Graham Tempest is a British-American author who divides his time between Oxfordshire and Florida.

GrahamTempest.com